Metamorphose V1

2015

Metamorphose

Project Editor: Tammy Davies

Assistant Editor: Kaitlyn Peer

Logo and Cover Design: Mary Davisson

V 1 Stories

Introduction from the Editor

EVERYONE LOVES STORIES. WHETHER as a reader, writer, or just someone who likes regaling tales of weekend adventures, there's a writer in all of us. And when that moment of inspiration strikes and we transform from a weekend fabler to aspiring author, something within us changes. There's a driving need to create something truly wonderful and share it with the world. But also, a need for validation.

For most aspiring authors, the hardest part isn't necessarily getting published. It's figuring out why it isn't happening. After all, there's a brilliant story there. Why is it getting rejected?

As Senior Editor, my job isn't just to select stories and toss them together for publication. I hunt for stories by the same authors who find rejections overwhelming and help them answer that nagging question: Why? I see what other editors don't. I discover stories with promise; stories that just need a nudge in the right direction to help them reach their fullest potential. By the end of the editing process, almost every author I work with offers kind words of thanks, because I didn't just clean their story. I helped them find those weaknesses in their writing which result in rejection. Some have since moved on to further publication or book deals.

There is nothing more rewarding. I feel truly blessed in what I do.

This year, we are proud to feature our very first Best Online Story, "Burn the Witch". It far surpassed our expectations for the most hits, shares, and likes.

The 2016 Metamorphose Writing Contest was a smashing success. We had so many great submissions it was difficult to choose only a handful. In the end, our selections were made based on an overarching theme to support the great stories.

Metamorphose V1 dives into the psyche of humanity. How our actions define our past and future. How we need to be blind to our differences and accept each other for the greater good. How darkness can overtake us all. How greed motivates our actions. How helplessness creates doubt. In their own way, each story asks the question: How will your actions define you when the darkness comes?

Spread the word of these brilliant authors to your friends and family, and encourage them to purchase a copy as well.

My hope is that Metamorphose continues to help authors transform their work into rewarding careers in science fiction and fantasy. I want to spread their words and gain them wider exposure. I want to offer them a bridge into publishing. But crossing that bridge also requires you, the reader. So thank you for purchasing this issue, and ask you to leave a review on Amazon, Goodreads, or anywhere else you wish. Because these authors need **you** to succeed.

Sincerely,
Tammy Davies
Senior Editor

Passio

Peter Krumpe

CLEOPATRA AND RICHARD THE Third were going at it. From his window, Oliver could hear the squeaks as Cleopatra drove her claws into the soft fur of her feeble lover. The sound of animal lust brought a smile to his lips. It meant the potion was working. The cool night air brushed his face, carrying with it the fragrance of the city street below. The aroma of hot dogs and fried food mixed with the musky smell of rainwater running down the dumpster behind his apartment and congealed into a pungent mist which made its way into his nasal passages. The sounds of the city were muffled by the rain outside his window. Car horns and loud New York voices were blotted out by the resounding pitter-patter of droplets hitting the glass pane.

The light from the hallway cast a line under the door. Oliver was alone in his apartment, save the three rats, Adonis, Cleopatra, and Richard the Third, who he'd rescued from the Chanel laboratory a week ago. In that lilac scented dungeon, rats were treated like cheap objects, used and discarded like tubes of toothpaste or disposable shaving razors. Oliver pitied the rats for this and had decided to smuggle them out of work in his lunch bag, making a pledge to the furry little critters that he would use them for one experiment and one experiment only before setting them free to run through the streets and sewers of Manhattan.

Adonis, the larger of the two males, whimpered from his cage as he watched his former mate make passionate love to the nefarious

Richard the Third. Richard was a runt, and as he mounted Cleopatra, the disfigured leg from which he got his name wiggled, trying to find purchase in her white fur. Oliver walked to the cages and gave the rats their water. Norway rats mated for life, and up until thirty-six hours ago, Cleopatra had been Adonis's one and only. But through the subtle manipulation of chemical bonds, Oliver had pulled love up by the roots. Now, the once prideful Cleopatra had become Richard's whore.

Across the street, a twenty-foot Kate Upton crouched on a billboard, wearing a silk nightie and brandishing a vial of Chanel's new fragrance, "Passio". Oliver had been one of the top chemists behind the fragrance, but it was unlikely that his contribution would rise to the surface and become public knowledge. The true nature of Passio would remain concealed, buried beneath the massive ad campaign launched in the weeks leading up to Valentine's Day. And yet it was that hidden power—that secret science of Oliver's—which had brought the giant Kate Upton to her knees, clutching the potion like a priceless jewel.

Above the model's head was the word "Passio", written in black Times New Roman with a scarlet heart dotting the "I". When the company had given that name to his brainchild, Oliver was pissed. He wanted to speak out, to tell them that the name was unworthy of his creation, but it wasn't the place of a chemist right out of grad school to question his executives. So he suffered silently, cringing every time the name "Passio" was mentioned. The word was Latin for "passion," but it doubled as the Latin for "suffering" as well, a fact which Oliver assumed the advertising execs had overlooked.

Oliver's contribution, the defining aspect of the product, could be found on the outside packaging in almost microscopic print. Fucitol Cumene was the active ingredient that gave Passio its kick. This undetectable, odorless compound would elevate Passio to new heights and revolutionize the world of cosmetics. For it was not merely an external change that Fucitol Cumene brought about, but an internal one as well. Living in the age of transcendence, it seemed to Oliver to be the next logical step in cosmetic science. Why settle with altering the body when one could just as easily alter the soul? And so, the powerful aphrodisiac now known as Fucitol Cumene was synthesized and added to each vial of Passio, ready to be mass-produced and distributed to an unsuspecting public.

Studies had shown that women who wore the fragrance received fifteen percent more attention from potential suitors over the course of an evening than those who wore the leading brand. This finding became a central pillar of the marketing campaign. However, the ads failed to mention the fact that the women also showed a ten percent spike in serotonin and estrogen production while wearing the fragrance, resulting in heightened sex drive. It wasn't the sweet pineapple aroma that let women who wore Passio have more luck with men. It was the fact that it made them horny. A woman who wore Passio would sooner put herself out there. The tiny vial, sold in a pink box with a ribbon on it, would spawn a generation of sexually courageous women, ready to tackle the night with hormone-fueled zest.

Oliver smiled at the thought. In truth, he'd had been working on Fucitol Cumene for years. The thought of creating a real-life love potion had fascinated him ever since he was a homely youth. He wasn't particularly unattractive, but it was rare that he got any attention from the fairer sex. He had greasy, unmanageable hair and narrow shoulders. His teeth were slightly crooked, and when he smiled the tendons in his neck would press outward, highlighting his sinewy frame. It was because of his condition that he had created the extract which would now infiltrate the homes of women across America. He alone had changed the culture. He had corrected the balance between male and female as he saw it, and tonight it was time for him to reap the rewards. On his own, he had synthesized two hundred milliliters of Fucitol Cumene, ten of which were currently inside of Cleopatra's digestive system. The rest was in a vial in his pocket.

He walked over and looked at the rats. Cleopatra and Richard the Third had taken a break from their lovemaking. They had been going at it for hours and the creatures looked weak. Oliver paced around and took stock of his room. Everything had an order to it, a stark cleanliness that he wasn't used to. He sprayed Febreeze and moved the rat's cages into the closet. His apartment had to be perfect for when his date arrived.

The smell of soup wafted down the hall. Beef bouillon. He made his way to the kitchen and turned the stove down. At that moment, his phone lit up. It was a text from Jennifer:

I'm in the lobby.

Oliver's palms began to sweat. Jennifer was a good friend of his whom he'd met in grad school. Ever since their first interaction, Oliver knew he was in love with her. Sadly, the feelings had never been reciprocated. Instead, he became the crying shoulder; the friend she got coffee with when her latest relationship didn't work out.

Yet despite her revolving door of insincere boyfriends, Oliver saw her as the epitome of virtue. She had a magnanimous nature that he respected and, in some senses, envied. Whereas Oliver's motivation for working at Chanel was less than pure, Jennifer had gotten a job as an environmental scientist for a waste management company right out of grad school. Oliver wasn't surprised. Preserving the world was right up her alley. While he schemed and manipulated, she devoted herself to cleaning an unclean world. It was this morally upright woman whom he would try to corrupt tonight. Inside her beautiful body, the wound which had festered within him would become diluted and purified. He buzzed her in. A few minutes later, she was at the door to his apartment.

"Oliver, it's been too long!" she said, entering his abode.

"Yeah, I know!" he smiled. "You look great." He added. He meant it too. She was wearing a black peacoat and had her hair in braids. As Oliver ushered her into the dining room, his mouth began to feel dry. "Sit down! Make yourself comfortable."

"Thank you," she said, hanging her coat on one of the chairs. The table was arranged delicately, with two red placemats opposite each other and a candle holder as a centerpiece. "So, what's the plan for tonight?" she asked.

"Well, I thought we could stay in for dinner and catch up. I've got soup on the stove."

"Sounds like a good call," she said. "It's raining pretty hard outside."

"Mm-hm," Oliver said. He'd made sure to schedule this dinner on an evening for which rain was forecasted. The two of them always made plans a week in advance, giving Oliver time to prepare. Jennifer liked order in her life, so Oliver had cleaned meticulously in preparation for her arrival, being sure to straighten out the books on his bookshelf and alphabetize his CD collection. Gray rugs lined the marble kitchen floor, and the frill on his scarlet seat cushions was a mustard yellow. On the kitchen counter was a sleek white iHome next to a banzai tree.

"I think the soup's actually about ready. I'll go get it," Oliver said, standing up. Jennifer made a move to follow him into the kitchen. "No no, you stay here. Make yourself at home."

She looked at him with mild bewilderment before settling back in her chair. "Whatever you say."

As Oliver walked to the kitchen, he felt a throbbing in his temples. He reached into his pocket and pulled out the vial. Jennifer called to him from the dining room.

"So, I hear you're working for Chanel now?"

"Yeah," he shouted back. He was transfixed by the small vial of Fucitol Cumene.

"What made you want to start working there?"

He began to ladle the soup into two bowls. "Oh, well it's honestly just a placeholder job right now. Until I can find something better," he lied.

"I only applied there because I knew somebody and I thought it would up my chances. Still, the pay's decent."

"Oh?" Oliver was glad he couldn't see her expression.

"Yeah. How's waste management? Still making the world a better place?"

"You'd be appalled at the waste people go through in this country. It's pretty depressing. I guess it's good job security though. I can always count on Americans to keep me employed."

Oliver strained to listen, but her voice became drowned out by the sound of his heart pounding against his ribcage. He uncorked the vial, which almost slipped through his sweaty fingers. Biting his lip, he poured the odorless potion into the broth and added a few extra pinches of salt. If what he was doing was wrong, it was for the right reasons. All he needed was one night. One night of unbridled passion and she would wake up knowing that he was the right man. One night, and after that he would never use the potion again. This was the promise he made to himself.

He tossed the vial in the recycling and returned to the dining room, carrying the bowls of soup. "Dinner is served. Dig in."

He handed Jennifer her bowl and watched her as she took a sip. "Ooh, not bad!" she said.

"Thank you." He chuckled nervously. "So, enough about work. How have you been? I want to hear about your life."

The two of them conversed at length. Once Jennifer got started, she could go on for hours. She talked about movies, art, and books she'd read, but thankfully never brought up a new boyfriend. Oliver monitored her closely for any sign that the potion was taking effect, counting the number of times she bit her lips or reached to fix her hair. He'd read articles online which said that such movements indicated physical attraction, but in truth, he had no way of distinguishing them from normal physical ticks. He had no point of reference by which to measure flirtation. Any and all results were inconclusive.

A half-hour later, she finished her soup. "That was a delicious meal," she said, smiling at him.

"I'm glad you liked it. Do you want dessert? I've got strawberries and powdered sugar."

"Ooh, fancy!" she said. Her eyes were locked onto his, and he noticed that she was tilting her head slightly to the side. "Is this how you always dine or are you giving me the special treatment?"

Oliver laughed. "I don't know," he said, swallowing.

He walked the kitchen, wiping beads of sweat from his forehead. Jennifer was acting different. It was a subtle change, but she had more confidence. Her words had a sweeping swagger to them, a relaxed bravado. He took a deep breath and returned to the dining room holding a plate full of strawberries and a leaf-shaped bowl that held powdered sugar.

"Ooh la la," Jennifer said. "You really know how to treat a lady."

Oliver stood there, frozen in place.

"What's the matter? You look like you've seen a ghost."

He laughed. "I, uh... I just need to go to the bathroom," he said. He tried to keep a steady hand as he placed the strawberries on the table before hurrying towards his room, which had an adjoining lavatory. "Be back in a minute."

He scurried into the bathroom, and looked in the mirror. "Here you go Oliver," he said. "Are you ready?" He was equal parts horny and terrified. If he went through with this, would it really be Jennifer he was sleeping with? She was flirting with him, that much was certain. But was it really just due to the extract? Perhaps the Fucitol Cumene had merely unlocked a side of her that she'd always had, but had buried deep down. As he formulated these thoughts, a new smell made its way to his nostrils.

It was subtle at first, but distinct. It smelled musky, kind of like rotten food. The odor perplexed Oliver, who'd been careful to keep his room spick and span in preparation for tonight. He went out into the bedroom and tried to locate its origin, looking under the bed and in the trash. Had he left food lying around? He didn't remember ever eating in here. He was about to give up and return to the kitchen when he realized that the smell was coming from the closet.

Hesitantly, he opened the closet door. What he saw made him want to throw up. Cleopatra was lying dead on her back, blood gushing from her ear. Adonis ran in circles around his cage, while Richard the Third curled up in the corner, somehow terrified by the body he'd been so enamored of. Oliver lowered a hand in and plucked the dead rat off the ground. She was cold. There were no external wounds, but the veins around her eyes bulged outwards, and a faint trickle of blood poured from her ear.

Jennifer's voice called from the dining room. "If you don't come back soon, I'm gonna have to come find you!" Oliver's throat was dry. He was in shock.

"One minute," he wheezed back.

He closed his eyes, hoping to god that what he saw would burn itself from his retinas, but he could feel the body of the rat in his hand. It occurred to him that if Jennifer saw the thing she'd be repulsed, so he ran to his drawer, pulled out a white sock, and stuffed the creature inside. He then threw it in the cage and shut the closet. Wiping his hands, he took a deep breath and tried to move past what had just happened.

"Come on, I'm waiting," called Jennifer. Oliver swallowed, then walked down the white hallway and into the dining room.

"There you are," she said. Her red lips curled upward, forming a playful smirk. Nearly all of the strawberries had been eaten. "I thought I'd have to come in and get you." She motioned to the seat next to her and he sat down. She was holding a tiny statue of a werewolf, which she'd taken off of Oliver's shelf. "Do you remember this?"

Oliver remembered. It was from the day they'd spent in Illinois. Oliver's friend Jay smelted metal at Granite City Works and had offered to give them a tour of the steel mill. At the end of the tour, they made statues by melting lead in a steel pot and pouring the silver liquid into molds of Halloween characters. The only sets they had were Halloween characters and birds so Oliver got a wolfman, Jennifer got a mummy, and Jay—who was a bird enthusiast—got a white-crowned sparrow. The statues were bright silver.

He exhaled a sigh of relief. "Yeah, of course I remember. What did you make again?" he asked, knowing the answer.

"I made a mummy," she said. "That was a fun day. We should do things like that more often." Oliver didn't respond. Something wasn't right. Jennifer shifted slightly closer in her chair and leaned forward, chin up, looking directly into his face. He wasn't used to her gaze. "You know, I was thinking while you were back there..." She gestured to his room. "And I realized that I've been awfully ungrateful to you."

"Oh?" Oliver swallowed. "How so?"

"For all that you do! You take me to nice places. You cook me dinner. You are reliable and trustworthy and always there for me. That's really special. It isn't often that you meet someone who's so altruistic."

A tear dripped down Oliver's face.

"Aw, don't cry," she said, putting her hand on his leg and gently massaging his thigh. "Look at me. You're a beautiful man."

Oliver wiped his tears and obeyed. There was something mesmerizing in her stare; something so beautiful and calming that for a second Oliver knew what it was to feel bliss. Then her expression glazed over, and a slight twitch began to send tremors through her lower lip. Her eyes became bloodshot, as if they were possessed by some insatiable hunger. "Jennifer are you okay?" Oliver asked.

"Yeah," she chuckled. "I actually feel great."

"Oh, that's good." He gulped.

"In fact," she said, moving her hands closer to his crotch, "I haven't felt this good in a while."

He reared backward. "Wait, what are you doing?"

"What we both want me to." She reached for him.

"No!" he shouted out and sprang to his feet. He couldn't bring himself to look at her. She was too vile, too rat-like in her expression.

"What's the matter?" she said, standing up.

"I...I don't want to compromise our friendship."

She laughed. "Don't be silly. Now come here." She extended her hand.

"Jennifer, I'm a virgin!" he blurted out.

For a moment Jennifer stopped. Then she smiled. "That's okay, baby. We can take it slow."

Oliver reveled in horror at the sudden and complete change in her being. The woman he'd loved had been morphed into a hideous caricature of a male fantasy. As she stepped towards him, he screamed and ran into his bedroom, locking the door behind him. The rain outside was coming down hard on the windowpane. A putrid smell filled the room, wafting out of his closet.

"Oliver!" she shouted through the door.

"Go away!"

"Come on, let me in. You're being ridiculous."

"No, no, no!" he shrieked.

She pounded on the door. "I just want to talk!"

"Get out of here!"

There was a brief pause before she spoke again. "Is it that you don't find me attractive? Is that it, Oliver?"

Oliver's heart sank. Was it not enough that he had poisoned the poor woman? He sighed. "No, I think you're very attractive."

There was silence from the other side of the door.

"Jennifer?"

He was considering opening it when the pounding resumed. "Then let me in, you fucking tease!" she shrieked.

He ran the bed and covered his ears with a pillow. Even with the sound muffled, he could still hear her screaming and pounding at the door. He closed his eyes and began to cry. He had accomplished what he'd set out to do. The energy between male and female had been balanced.

It was an hour before the pounding finally stopped. Oliver waited ten more minutes, then cracked the door ever so slightly. He cautiously ventured out into the hallway. Jennifer's coat was no longer on the chair, and the door to his apartment was open. Oliver returned to his window and looked out into the rainy night. It would be a while before he could sleep.

OLIVER CALLED IN SICK the next two days. When he returned to work on Wednesday, his boss had an assignment for him. Chanel's next fragrance "Aurora", which was set to be released in August, was toxic and had caused the lab rats to become inebriated. Oliver's task was straightforward: identify the caustic agent and remove it from the formula, or at least remove enough to significantly lower the toxicity. He had just set up a microscope with a petri dish of the sample and a small tube full of solvent when he was approached by his coworker Brian, with whom he'd gone to grad school.

"Hey man, do you remember Jennifer Summers?"

Oliver's throat clenched. "Yeah. Why do you ask?"

"Man, I'm sorry to tell you this. I don't know if you were friends with her or not, but she died on the L train a few nights ago."

"That's terrible!" said Oliver, putting a hand over his mouth. His heart sank as though it were full of lead.

Brian nodded. "They say that she had a stroke. Nobody knows what caused it."

"Oh my god."

"But get this. Before she died, she was seen prowling the subways around midtown. Like ten people came forward and said that she'd approached them asking for sex."

"That's crazy! I can't believe that," said Oliver, knowing full well it was true.

"Yeah, it's weird. You'd expect that kind of shit from a man, but not a woman. Especially one as good-looking as her. I guess she must've been pretty desperate for a hookup."

Oliver shook his head and glanced down at the poisons he was playing with. "Just when you think you know someone."

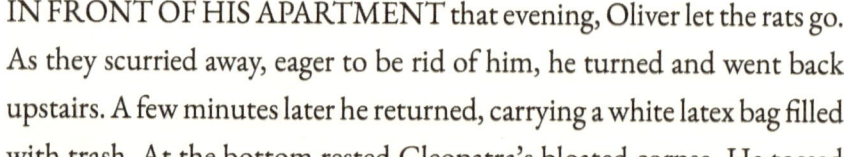

IN FRONT OF HIS APARTMENT that evening, Oliver let the rats go. As they scurried away, eager to be rid of him, he turned and went back upstairs. A few minutes later he returned, carrying a white latex bag filled with trash. At the bottom rested Cleopatra's bloated corpse. He tossed it in the dumpster and wiped his hands on his jeans. He'd try very hard to forget this incident.

The setting sun cast streaks of amber light onto the skyscrapers. The steady hum of the city would continue well into the night. Across the street, the giant Kate Upton wore a forced smile.

PETER KRUMPE is a recent graduate of Muhlenberg College with a major in English and a double minor in Philosophy and Creative Writing. He enjoys reading fantastical epics like "Dune" or "The Stand,"

but also loves cerebral novels which focus on troubled or isolated characters. Peter craves outdoor activity, be it hiking, cycling, running, or just traipsing around the wilderness. His drug of choice is philosophical conversations with friends over coffee.

Missing Jack Diderot

David Halliday

AUGUST 26. 7:35 A.M. 2012

A figure stood alone in the morning heat, silent among the crickets, dim and insubstantial in the oscillating heat of a slow-cooking day. In the strangeness of the light his outline, though hazy and nebulous, soon become quick with clarity.

I watched mutely and regarded the wanderer with skepticism. The figure represented an unsettling transit from myth to actuality; he who was an idea, was now a living being. A thing of mass, with an apple-red heart thudding wetly in a fleshy body.

As he raised his face, I cupped my eyes, heart hammering, hand resting on the doorframe.

THIRTY YEARS EARLIER: AUGUST 26. 7:35 a.m. 1982

In the closing days of summer, 1982, the skies were luminous and clear. At dawn, on the grass and budding fronds of the apple tree, beaded dew would glow amber in the morning sun like tiny balls of molten iron.

Summers were geological eras, their epochs marked with entire campaigns, rises and falls, complete with its own great loves and great tragedies. Seasons were divided into their own measures of years. I expected our final year of high school to last decades.

Jack was a new student in the senior class, with hair the color of walnut meat, smooth skin, and eyes denim blue. He was new, and everything new belonged to us. In a world of greens and golds, we believed that, unlike the Frost poem, everything gold could stay.

Jack Diderot smiled with a fair measure of sadness, as though his smile meant something very profound. Like he was sitting on a gurgling well of secrets. Of course, I feel pulled into saying that now, into crouching by his image in supplication. You always lace people's words with gravity once they are gone.

I first saw him sitting alone in homeroom. Sweeping cropped bangs from my eyes, I instantly forgot why I'd spent the morning deliberating which thick necklace and sagging black sweater combo would be best to kick off the school year.

No one knew much about him. Like any new arrival in a town unconvinced of its own significance, it only took a handful of conversations for rumors to begin: of his being the smartest, the shyest, the most aloof; that he was cool, or that he was not. Those who ventured to know him reported that he was orphaned at an early age; that he lived with his aunt and uncle on a property just outside of town.

Jack's looks would interrupt conversations. The girls, myself included, were intrigued until they found out how shy he was. With a face like that, they expected James Dean nonchalance, a Joe Strummer attitude; a cliché of frowns and narrowed squints into somewhere far away. But he was something rare that didn't seem to belong in a town where the civic religion was high school football, and the messiah was the QB-1.

In the corridors, Jack would see cheerleaders with their lopsided Cyndi Lauper hair and footballers in varsity letter jackets. Yet he never seemed to pay them their due, as would be typical for any newcomer prostrating themselves for social currency. And that intrigued me. The ruling class of the football noblesse d'épeé didn't rank a mention in his small, strange world.

When it came to boys as a genre, there weren't many subdivisions for a girl to choose from. It was all cans of Miller and riding in pickup trays doing laps of Main Street. So when I spotted Jack, I decided to go on safari and hunt him down.

Ultimately, my life history of Jack Diderot was a question of weeks. They were weeks of burgers, Chinese food, and endless cigarettes and refills of filter coffee, and at the time it didn't seem to mean much.

THE BLEACHERS: SEPTEMBER 30. 7:35 p.m. 1982

The sun slanted through a bank of clouds. A bird of prey swooped low to the ground, arced up suddenly, and then landed flapping in the silver bough of a birch, low and close to where we sat in the grass. The bird cried out in a brassy clearing of its vocal pipes.

"Merlin," Jack said.

I turned to Jack, a hand to my face. "What?"

"Merlin. Type of falcon," he whispered. "Eats other birds that it catches in midair. One of the fastest animals on earth. When it dives, it just... disappears."

"Lucky. Smart move in a town like this." I took a menthol from a cigarette pack and dangled it from my lips. I tilted the box towards him. "Cigarette?"

He shook his head. I lit up and picked a stray hair off my tongue. Then I examined my Doc Martens, smooth and layered in a film of dust. Perfect moments never seem that way when you're in them, I thought.

After school, we spent the afternoon walking. In a desert town, for those who didn't like sleeping with footballers, there was little to do except walk, smoke, and listen to the radio. We eventually circumnavigated the fields and ovals back to the school, the halfway point between our two houses. We dawdled and lingered there often.

I wanted to take his hand, but part of me believed I never would. I wasn't the sort of person who deserved a Jack Diderot. The fact that we spent time together still astounded me sometimes.

In the paling light of an afternoon by the football field on the bleachers, the air was hazy and indistinct, like the beginnings of a light fog. Voices sounded close. "Everything is so beautiful here. Complete, you know?" he said. "I heard that happiness consists of recognizing that this is all a great strange dream... Where things happen as they were meant to happen. Like Blake: Some were born to endless night."

He walked with a copy of The Way of a Pilgrim sticking out of his back pocket.

"Is that from your book?" I asked.

He shook his head.

"What's the book about, then?"

He didn't answer immediately. "I think purification. The writer, this anonymous monk, says: 'My final purification is complete. I am pure, perfect, and ready for the stars.' I love that."

"Where do you find this stuff?" I blew minted smoke into the sinking sun.

As soon as I got home I scribbled these words down on a yellow notebook I kept in a bedside drawer. I stared at the sentence in my blue rollercoaster scrawl, and the words had a weight of significance I could only guess at. Even then I cherished anything that gave insight into Jack. I flipped through my notebook containing pages of scrawled notes of things he said. I'd stuck other scraps of paper, like receipts and torn newsprint to the pages. Every time he mentioned a band or an artist, play or film, I would quickly find a scrap of paper and scribble it down. My yellow notebook was my Book of Jack.

THE DISAPPEARANCE: SEPTEMBER 30. 8:05 p.m. 1982

Late that afternoon Jack left for home, walking across the football field before sundown. His hair was glorious and golden as the sun bled its orange over the hills. His canvas sneakers scrabbled dry against the dirt track behind the bleachers. I supposed he had an errand because the highway road he took ran perpendicular to the one that would have taken him home.

Over my shoulder I watched his darkening figure drawn into space, cutting across fields. I buttoned up my jacket and spied a clump of blue material draping itself over a rusted white rail in the bleachers like one of Dali's clocks. Jack left it. I turned to look for him, but he was nowhere.

I left the denim jacket melting on the bleachers railing for a slow fifteen minutes. It was easy to think he would return for it.

Eventually, I lifted the jacket and let it hang from my arm. His was the last skin the fabric had touched, made soft against his heat. I patted the pockets to see if he had left a wallet; something that would increase the urgency with which I needed to return to him. The jacket was loose and empty, except the inner pocket. There I found a silver coin bearing strange symbols that looked like some runic, foreign script. I turned the coin over in my hand feeling its weight, then returned it to the pocket.

That night, hunters' fires spotted the dark like sparkling ghosts.

The next day, Jack was not in school. In the morning, the homeroom teacher read out his name, a little louder than the class milieu. "Diderot? Jack?" with a rising intonation. The teacher's head swiveled, inquiring of the various faces with his eyebrows, read the name again, this time as a question. "No?", then he would move on to the next name. Donaldson, then Gilford, then Graham, then Kelly.

I figured Jack was late, or maybe took the morning off. He was strange like that, and I wouldn't put it past him.

But Jack was absent the day after, and the day after, without a word. Jack Diderot was not at lunch, he was not at assembly. He would not go to his locker, he would not remove his bag, he would not clang the door shut. His canvas sneakers would not squeak on the linoleum floors, they would not step nimbly over smears of squished apple, they would not incidentally kick balls of scrunched lined paper. His pupils would not dilate as he stepped into the sun from the halls.

Still, I scanned every crowd for his face, his flaxen hair. I became quick and thorough: skilled at examining crowds at a glance to ascertain where he was not.

It was only once he was gone I realized the ways Jack had colored my days, and exactly how much pleasure could be found in the presence of another.

I would turn Jack's coin over in my fingers, carefully trying to decipher its mysteries. I would puzzle over the secrets it held as one of the last relics of Jack. I would hold it delicately in my palm and fingertips until it grew hot, and took to kissing it lightly before sleep. I researched all runes and foreign scripts but could find nothing to match the script pressed deep in the coin's surface. Those nights in the following weeks, the Pleiades rested above the horizon, sailing from Orion's relentless pursuit. I watched the stars arc across heaven and extinguish themselves into the inky world. In the moonlight, I was a strange and solitary tribeswoman forged in silver, reading futures the night skies.

THE WATCH: OCTOBER 15. 5:05 p.m. 1982

Police are loath to open an investigation when it comes to missing young men. Young men leave. Maybe they didn't want to be married or hated their job or went to make their fortunes in a bigger city. Any of the multiple reasons why men choose to escape. Police had that same reluctance with Jack Diderot. They would keep an eye out, they said.

It wasn't until Jack's watch was found that interest peaked.

A farmhand named Chris Kawalski had been driving along the interstate in his sky-blue GMC pickup. Around 5:05 p.m. his car battery gave out. He walked half a mile to the Texaco where he picked up a new one. Kawalski lugged it back to his truck, trudging in the grass through clefts of indigo shade, his hair sweaty under his cap. While walking, he'd seen a silver thing lodged in a nest of grass twenty feet away. It was the corner of a Casio watchband, silver and stretchable. He picked it up, snorted, and slipped it in his trouser pocket.

This discovery almost went unnoticed. The following day, Chris Kawalski told his friend Buddy Gaynor about the watch while sitting at the counter of the diner over a lunch of pecan pie and coffee. Gaynor turned the broken watch over in his hands.

In the diner, I sat alone over a chocolate malt. From my position in a booth, I watched them huddling together over coffee like conspirators.

Gaynor convinced his friend to turn the watch in to the police after studying the copperplate initials engraved behind the watch's face. At police stations, items are logged, checked against lost property records, and stored for a finite period of time. Kawalski was allowed to take it after a week if no one claimed it.

I don't need to say that in our town—in any small town—news travels fast. That evening, Buddy Gaynor allegedly told his girlfriend about Kawalski's find, the story deeply enmeshed somewhere inside a granola bar of mundane information about his day. Gaynor's girlfriend, Sheree Patterson, was an intern at the local tabloid, The Star. She'd heard about Jack, the missing boy. Eager for an opportunity to establish herself, Sheree saw the story and thought it worth forcing the connection between Jack and foul play. The thought twisted itself around in my stomach like a parasitic worm.

THE INVESTIGATION: OCTOBER 21. 2:05 p.m. 1982

Within the week, Jack's picture was printed on the side of one-liter milk cartons, black and white and grinning.

The police took Kawalski to point out roughly where he'd seen the watch. He couldn't be sure. But he was giddy with the attention the watch had brought him. As a sort of repayment, he approached the task with more grim solemnity than anything he'd done in recent memory. He tried his best to replicate the event exactly, even though he had forgotten the particulars.

Jack's Aunt Nance and Uncle Hud were taken into custody and questioned. They were called back to the station for three days straight. In interviews for The Star, they entreated the community for information. Jack's aunt was weepy and frail, quivering like a sick lamb.

I was taken in and questioned. The officer I spoke to looked no older than my classmates. I told him I sat with Jack on the bleachers that day. I recounted exactly what we'd spoken about. The falcon. The book. Purification. What did he mean? I didn't know. I told them I watched him walk home via an unusual route. That he forgot his jacket.

"Seen any suspicious characters?"

"I don't know. No."

On the day of his disappearance, Jack had been spotted speaking with a man outside the Arby's. The man had been well dressed and drove a black Lincoln. A server at the Arby's testified that they'd spoken for maybe five minutes. Jack had pointed along a back road disappearing into desert, like he was giving directions.

With poignant equanimity, the investigating officer pressed on with his questions, cutting a rough shape of the situation.

When it was too uncomfortable to consider the alternatives any longer, people at school tended to think that he ran away. An orphan, some said, was more likely prone to wandering. Maybe he felt the pull of the wild, like many other boys had before him. It was not uncommon, the police officer said, especially for young men. Maybe he'd given the watch away.

The fliers were thin white and pastel green A4 sheets. The picture was grainy, with high contrast. Some students passed them up over the town over two weekends. The long windows of the diner. The notice board in front of the school, where fliers were three deep and scaly with old tape. Lamp posts by the grocer's. The whitewashed walls outside the supermarket and the notice board inside.

The degree of hope was inversely proportional to the weeks that crawled by. Each week heaved itself over the next, lumbering into the night like a dying dog.

A reporter who must have been in his twenties asked, "Had he acted differently before he disappeared?" When pressed, a cheerleader decided he kept to himself more than usual. She stuck to this with the fervent support of two friends. Together they were satisfied they could offer something to the inquiring press while the subject was hot and relevant.

It seemed everyone had seen Jack somewhere.

A friend had seen him step on a bus with a man in his thirties with a tattoo on his left forearm, a man never accounted for. In the first few days, people thought he'd taken a Greyhound somewhere. New York. Los Angeles. Nashville. New Orleans. After that first week, speculations gained more attention, the focus of more town personalities aiding momentum. It became a town pastime.

I watched the news crew, watched the smiling teenagers take on airs of solemnity. Like there had been a school shooting. I watched and turned to the plains. There was a banked wall of cloud to the south as big as I imagined the finger of God, stretched over the firmament.

There was a video camera, a shabby-looking news van parked on municipal grass. It was a clear afternoon smeared by cirrus clouds when a small NBC regional news crew covered the story of the missing boy.

Boys had disappeared before. But I suppose it was a slow week, and this was a disappearance that bore the scent of the mysterious. I overheard a reporter mention murder and abduction in one breath.

The technicians set up the lights. The anchor stood with the façade of the James Madison High school in the background. A woman from the makeup department padded the glare from the anchor's face with a circle cotton pad. Cameraman Diego Cuspa counted her in. In only three takes, Melanie Nixon delivered lines fed by her producer.

"I'm standing in front of the James Madison High where it's day twenty of the disappearance of Jack Diderot. There's been no trace of Jack, except for a silver watch, cracked and stopped at precisely 8:05 pm, the exact time he was seen last by fellow student Aimee Chambers.

The watch was found roadside by the interstate, and authorities say it's the first sign of possible foul play. If you have any information on the whereabouts of Jack Diderot, please contact your local law enforcement authority. Melanie Nixon, NBC News."

That night, the air was full of fog and phantoms.

As a student, Jack was almost a stranger. But in those first few weeks, Jack Diderot had become everyone's favorite missing person. An erstwhile golden boy is made only that much more golden. The pastors of all the local churches prayed for him, for a speedy return, that the Lord's hand might be upon him, that he might be unharmed: If it's your will, Father. You search for your lost sheep, you leave the ninety-nine and search for the one that left the flock. Keep him in your hand. Guide his steps. Bring him home to us. Amen.

When four weeks had passed, the prayers lost their significance and were demoted to a passing mention in a medley of prayer at each service end. Congregations were asked to remember Jack Diderot and hold his family in their hearts. The First Methodist, the Grace Community Chapel, Saint Barnabas Presbyterian. They all mentioned their favorite almost-prodigal son. For a time.

Did Jack think the town would embrace him thus? Could he have guessed? Did he know what years of grief he had gifted to us? To me?

His too-often Xeroxed face on fliers became a sort of year-long Christmas decoration, there until they became embarrassing. It was strange to think that a smile could only exist on paper and memory; those perfectly white canines peeking through his lips rendered obsolete.

Very quickly, Jack's status underwent several noticeable changes. He went from friend to victim to curiosity. Whenever he came up in conversation those first few weeks, the question was always where. After where was always why.

White fliers became crisp and tea-colored. Edges warped into waves, corners curled and tore. Clear tape turned amber, dried, and flaked off.

Weekly World News ran a two-hundred-word article on Jack Diderot and cited alien abductions. But for a publication where allegations of the surreal were like bread and butter, no one paid much mind. After that, Jack Diderot became a statistic and outwardly seemed forgotten. His home became a soon-forgotten file in a police database somewhere.

But the heart is drawn to mystery. I suppose no one forgot that, in a town where people threw groceries into the trays of burgundy Ford pickups and listened to Hank Williams and John Cougar, a boy called Jack Diderot had disappeared one day and left his silver watch. Yet the patterns of lives continued, mundane.

Did people still think of Jack? Did the grocer? The butcher? The waiters at the Korean restaurant? Jack visited my thoughts daily and set me apart in time. Like a dying ember in a world of ash that had no knowledge of fire.

After Jack, I exiled myself from the world I knew. I finished school, didn't go to prom, and when graduation came I didn't bring a camera. I completed an English degree in a local college and wondered whether Jack would have done the same. The friends who I left said I needed to get out. That the town was leeching me dry of life before I'd done any living. And so I moved interstate for a part-time admin position with an academic publisher in Chicago. Away from Jack. Away from the school. Away from the desert buttes and eerie wind-carved rock formations.

I thought of Jack no less, wondering what he would make of the windy city, what he would listen to, where he would go. Everything I did was through a filter of Jack.

I lasted three years. When I returned, I took a job working in the library of the high school I had once attended. The same school Jack had spent his final days. Every brick pathway, every meeting place, every bench, every notice board was permanently etched with the memory of Jack Diderot.

I looked for physical evidence that he had once been there. Maybe he scratched his name into a desk or a bench. Maybe he'd signed some old canvases lost in an art class cupboard. Maybe he scribbled some notes in a book. I never found anything. The absence of clues made me hang on to the strange coin all the more tightly, as though it might grant me some answer or reason if I kept it close enough.

Missing someone enough is about bringing a part of those lost into the world again. If no one misses them when they're gone, it's no different to their never existing at all. So I built an altar to memory, in a place where forgetting Jack Diderot was impossible. In every seat of the cafeteria, I wondered whether it was one of the ones he'd sat in. I figured he'd probably sat on 15-20 percent of them in his time, and so at least once every week I came as close to physical contact with Jack as anyone alive.

I heard no fresh news of Jack so I stopped asking, as everyone had stopped asking long before me. After the news quelled, and the ripples of our community puddle began to fade, people began to treat me with a certain deference. After several failed attempts, they gave up tempting me with the trivial doings of the world or offers of their company, as had been my life formerly.

At night the shapes of the buildings were cold ash against a sky of fire. All cries of all lost children rose emptily into the silence of the world.

THIRTY YEARS LATER: AUGUST 26, 7:37 a.m. 2012

The figure raised its face. I stood with my heart thudding in my temples, a hand resting on the doorframe.

In the Parable of the Lost Son, I was always struck by the line: And the father ran out to meet him. I clasped the figure about the neck. Strange gagging sobs broke from my throat. After a time, with stings of spit bridging my lips, I said, "I have your jacket."

Jack stood before me, neither dusty nor travel-worn. In the early evening, the west Texas plains hinted at infinity.

I was silent, for we were now standing on holy ground. In the field by the house, I finally held him out by the shoulders. "Where have you been? Where have you been?" My breath held fast in my chest when I saw him close: Jack's skin was still taut, his eyes still shades of unwashed denim, deep factory blue. His t-shirt still burning white, his jeans, his sneakers, his hair, his teeth. It was all unchanged. Jack Diderot had not aged a day.

He said nothing. Nothing about my drooping mauve cardigan, nothing about my shapeless floral print dress, nothing about my crow's feet and under-eye bags. I wanted to apologize for aging the way I had.

The wings stopped flapping in my chest, but it was minutes before I spoke again.

"I've waited for you." You don't know how I've waited, I thought. Thirty years. I've seen thirty years. In those thirty years, I can't come up with a course that might explain you standing before me now. I had not thought of how the skin unsmooths itself over the passage of decades. To my sudden shame, mine no longer fit my body as it once had done.

What created this laceration in time? What invisible violence absented him from us? We crossed the field back towards the house and stepped up the low wooden stairs. The porch was illuminated softly by tangerine lamplight.

"Are you real?" I said. "How are you here like this? How are you here?"

He was quiet, and when he spoke he formed words slowly and his voice crackled like dry paper. "The same reason you are," he said. His voice was similar; high and gentle. Rougher than it was. He looked bewildered and flighty.

"What reason?"

"Reason..." he said, looking around, as though dazed. "You're here, living out your days. Maybe unburdened by purpose or decision. Or reason."

"I don't need a reason to be here. I haven't been missing for thirty years."

There was something careful about him. "Missing?" he said, as though trying to recall something at the edge of memory.

I felt my face pull into a frown. His ignorance of his own tragedy made me want to disintegrate into sorrow. "Thirty years." You don't know how I've waited, I thought. I passed over a lifetime, waiting for you.

"Are you sure?"

"Positive."

"That's why you look older than you did yesterday," he said. "I was gone?"

"Gone."

"And you remembered me all that time. And now I'm back." He wanted to know what year it was. I told him. At which point he asked again. "I'm back," he repeated, eyes wandering dreamily. It was as though for him no time had passed at all, and he was no more than a senior student on the butt end of an elaborate practical joke. "I'm back for some reason, maybe one not my own..." Then his attention seemed to clarify and his gaze fixed on me. "I forgot something. You have my jacket?"

I nodded. "But are you real?"

"As real as I ever was."

I paused. "Where have you been?" It wasn't quite an accusation.

"I don't know how to answer that," he said.

"You left. Just when I was beginning to need you. I needed you around. Why weren't you around?" He was quiet and looked at me. He clasped his hands into a knot and began rubbing a knuckle against his lower lip. The muscles of his forearm were still cable tight.

"What happened to you?"

"I don't know. I walked. Home from the bleachers, across the hills at dusk. Then when I forgot my jacket, I turned to walk to your place."

"And?"

"And here I am."

"Did you die?" I said.

"I don't think so."

I learned that mysteries determine a person's steps, as much as anything else. No one can understand the reasons that picked them up and dropped them anywhere. At that moment, Jack unwittingly revealed that the world is governed by strange games, in the movement of everything, and behind everything. With impenetrable codices of rules that stretch back to the very beginning.

"Also," he said, "I lost my watch."

The day grew warm and seemed to pass in a haze. I convinced him that I needed to call the police if just to cross off another name on their missing person's list. He was dreamy and unperturbed. Early that afternoon, police took him to the station for questioning. I wondered about how the officers would phrase the questions everyone was asking. I doubt they had any more success at coherence or believable solutions.

Jack was taken to the hospital where a doctor proclaimed him to be a perfectly healthy teenage boy. They kept him overnight for observation. Jack lay there the night through and explained nothing. I learned that explanations were elusive creatures.

While working at the library, I'd lived on a reading diet of heavily-thumbed novels of immortal passion like Wuthering Heights. Novels where love expands beyond all that is corporeal and domestic and burns like magnesium. I'd left my copy in the car so many times that it grew its own archipelagos of black mold in shades of green-black and purple on the inside cover.

It seemed the further the memory of Jack Diderot stretched from my icons of him, the more intense it became. My sadness grew. I consoled myself, saying it was a gift to see sadness so deep, that not everyone gets to see the ocean floor, to walk at the very bottom of a feeling.

Several nights following his return, I pulled a small leather-bound bible from the drawer of my bedside table. I pulled the ribbon to find my place in the Gospels. "They all realized they were in a place of holy mystery, that God was at work among them." Luke 7.11. My Jack Diderot, who once was lost now is found.

In a town of classmates whose skin was now marked and weathered like driftwood, who moved about with an age-induced slouch, in my mind I kept seeing Jack approach me upright, across a field at dawn.

Whenever he came up in conversation those first few weeks, people's glee quickly snapped to bafflement. The question was always how. After how was always where. Where had he been? Why had he not aged? How? Where had he been? Where had he been? Jack Diderot's last transition was from curiosity to culprit. When the fog surrounding his youth began to fade, the eyes of friends and strangers contracted with accusation. He was not missing at all. But no one could offer any suggestion that made any more sense than a Weekly World News article.

The Star made the same missteps as the townspeople and had initially rejoiced. They ran a lead double-page spread on the missing youth, the town poster boy who had miraculously returned unharmed after thirty years. The reporter, newcomer Rohan Kurtz from the Fredericksburg Standard, had not yet laid eyes on the prodigal son. He drove an egg-white Honda Civic to Jack's farm. Upon seeing Jack, he at once believed he had been taken for a sap. This boy, who could have been no older than eighteen, was not a man that had been missing from anywhere for thirty years. Kurtz blushed, conducted a short interview and drove away, vowing to never run a story on missing boys again.

Others who knew Jack saw through any accusation of hoax. For some, he became a pariah. His paper-smooth skin inspired subtle shades of jealousy in the crow-footed eyes of former classmates. Jack had been a high school golden boy. But for someone to stay fixed in that state for thirty years was not the behavior of a golden boy at all. Nothing gold can stay.

People said he died, and now somehow was made living. He was a day-lit ghost. Where there had been admiration soon left only suspicion.

Jack defied nature. How could something that defied the laws of nature be trusted? The barely civilized Texan wilderness had grown unaccustomed to hauntings. Living phantoms and changelings had slipped from the everyday awareness of the adoptive Walmart state.

When confronted with the god-like eternal youth of Jack, the town unanimously decided it preferred his memory. Townsfolk grew comfortable with the story of a missing boy and leaving the memory that way, as a deep pathos with no solutions. Maybe the promise of distant comfort if a body was ever found. If Jack had been struck down by a highway car and killed, that would have been a tragedy, but no conundrum. Now Jack was the pale Lazarus returning from some lower world, of which no tongue could utter.

In the weeks following his return, he said nothing of his ordeal. I would visit and catch him staring out the window—at the plains, always at the plains—and closing his eyes. Why? He had vanished into them once, in an instant stepping across an unseen threshold of thirty years.

Jack, you made us creep past you and almost shield our curious eyes in shame and horror. In a town of decay, you could not belong. We, the living, live in decay. In all our vehicles that rust, and pets that age and die, with food that spoils, all that decays is good.

JACK'S DENIM JACKET was still in a plastic Ziploc I'd once folded it in, resting in the bottom drawer. I slid it free carefully and laid it on the bed. I lifted it and sniffed it. The light denim smelled of dry must. I hung it on a coat hanger and hooked it around the door handle. The jacket was made alive in that hanging, and I took the sleeve and held it. It seemed emptier than it was.

I'd also kept the curious coin. The police had confiscated both for a time before returning them to Jack's uncle and aunt, who passed them on to me on the proviso I never washed the jacket. Back when the story was fresh, Jack's uncle Hud had driven over to my parent's house in a cherry-red Chevy, the jacket neatly folded on the passenger seat. Hud didn't say why he was giving it to me; just that he thought I might like to have it.

There was a live broadcast from the school that night, followed by a presentation in the town hall where Jack was welcomed home. On stage, the mayor shook his hand. Jack received a 'welcome home' prize basket wrapped in cellophane. Cameras flashed. Yet the celebrations seemed hollow and tainted by the foul odor of his untouched youth. It was a forced thing. Jack was looked upon by former classmates—now middle-aged—as a specter or demon when he might have been an angel.

After the presentation, I saw Jack only one more time. He appeared inside my house one day when all was quiet and I was heating tinned tomato soup in a saucepan. I had not heard him come in, yet there he was, standing in the doorway.

"It's time," he said. "I have to go."

"What? Where?"

To this, he said nothing, other than a glance over his shoulder out the kitchen window at masses of Texas stretching out to eternity.

"You need to tell me where. Are you in trouble? Are people after you? Tell me what's going on. We'll call the police. SWAT. FBI. The National Guard. Hell, we'll get a priest. Whoever you need. Just don't leave again. Please. We can make it work here. Don't leave again."

Jack stared out the window at the hills. In the early evening shadows you could make out faces in the rocky buttes and mesas. Like someone was watching our every movement. On the town outskirts, the land itself felt like a living presence. It was an ancient place where modern time, sense, and logic did not always apply and inexplicable things happened.

With his green eyes squinting from his unwrinkled face into the sun setting over a crumbling land, Jack said, "We both know I can't stay here. This isn't my time anymore."

"Then I'm coming with you. I'm not going to wait for you again. I'm not going to waste everything missing you again." I took his denim jacket from a peg in the hall. I took the coin in my hand and squeezed it in my palm until it felt white-hot.

The next morning, when the school librarian Karen Hamilton arrived for her mid-morning shift, she would find the building still dark with a ceiling fan flapping through the leaves of an open hardback edition of The Divine Comedy. She would realize I never showed up for my early morning shift. After calling to check why I was not at work and getting no answer, she would visit my house and find the door unlocked. She would push it open. Inside, the house would be cold.

Karen would call out softly as she tiptoed through the rooms. My keys would lie on the bench. She would peek in all rooms and find everything as it should be, not a paper out of place. Nothing that suggested I had been there recently except cold tomato soup, thick in the saucepan, and crimson spots of soup spilled on the kitchen linoleum floor. She would then exit, the sound of her footsteps creaking past quiet bookshelves stocked with hundreds of half-read volumes that would never be finished. Where would I be? When would I be? She would not know, but what she could guess mattered most is that I would be there with Jack.

Twenty-four hours later, Karen would make a police report, and in that soon-forgotten file, in the police database of unfinished stories, my name would take its place by Jack Diderot.

DAVID HALLIDAY is the Melbourne-based author of the non-fiction history The Bloody History of the Croissant. His short stories have appeared in Australia and the UK. In addition to receiving awards for screenwriting, his novella, "Heaven Opens," was shortlisted for the Busybird Great Novella Search. His feature articles have appeared in GQ, Huffington Post, and Foundr Magazine.

An Inexperienced Scholar of Bacchus

Vijay Johnson-Tanco

I SUPPOSE THE DETAILS of this weekend, without invasive censorship, should finally be unveiled. As for our character, the young Neil was comical, especially when the occasion called for his humor. Neil found that on certain such days he uncovered a delicate balance between pomposity and irony whenever he referred to himself in the third person.

The beginning of my trouble began Friday. I immediately woke up on the dot at 2:37 a.m. and directed myself to the fridge present at my dorm. The distance was the vast length of three feet, or 0.91 meters if you are not North American-centric. I retrieved my beverage to start the day, a hearty neon liquid by the brand of Mountain Slime. Do the Deed!

My roommate then kicked me out after drinking his regretful sludge. Where was a low Neil Feins to go on a sunny day like this? It must come as no surprise to you, dear reader, that my expansive list of friends (by my count four) were always there for me. Christina, a biology major on paper yet an English major by all other means, invited me to attend a party with her. Christina was one desperate for friends, I might add.

"Please Christina! Chrissy with a T! C-dog! Friend of my friends! I've never been to an actual casual party before like this!" Neil pleaded to his friend, who in turn shook her head.

"No. I told you this is only a party for close friends to my brother. You were the dick that bailed on him when he needed a bio partner." Christina stabbed her words into Neil's begging heart.

"Please Christina!" Neil complained. "I am so desperate to make new friends! My roommate keeps on stealing everything I have in the fridge."

"Not my problem."

"Please please please." Neil was practically on his hands and knees.

"I'm saying no." Christina remained resolute.

"Please? I can reimburse any damages."

"Fine," Christina gave in if for nothing else, to avoid any more of Neil's voice, who in turn celebrated in the best way he could: he offered his palm, hoping Christina would slap it back in that fashion that close friends would often do. Yet Christina parted without a word or mere acknowledgment, leaving Neil hanging with an upheld hand. Truly the best of friends.

Neil Feins, the suavest guy in all of University of Rakehurst. Did I ever mention that Neil Feins is pretty suave? There wasn't much to be said for the ambiance of the party. As it turns out, many college seniors are boring when they host college parties. As most people who attend this school realize, college parties are host to a gross amount of group debauchery, alcoholic liquids that freely flow to all red cups present, a plethora of games that almost always require the drinking of harmful liquids, impulsive pranks filled with regret, the free spirit of rebellion that injures so many students every weekend, and polite friendship and nothing more.

Speaking about making new friends, Neil Feins was the best. I'm sorry did I say the best? Because I actually meant the worst. Within the red cup I held was nothing but water, I assure you. No for real, I mean. Attention was on the nearby group of men lacking any shits, of course, bringing in the Buff. The Buff was unwashed and riddled brown, with clumps of feces mixed with dirt. Not the kind of brown common within healthy buffalo, but a brown that almost tarnished everything it meant to be an animal. The prospects of freedom, the pleasure of life, all are ridiculed and broken down by this same shade of stool. Never has an animal looked more pathetic, more depressed. And never have the games of an average college campus seemed so needlessly cruel. But the buzz prevalent within the minds of many young men convinced everyone else that this game of humiliation and brutality was nothing more than an activity to be shared with friends, and to impress possible mates for the night. On this night, nature has truly shown a remarkable majestic demeanor.

"Name of the game: upchuck roulette." It's here I must stop. I did promise to show my story without invasive censorship, but that is quite the pipe dream.

Spoilers.

The Buff, which we can all just call the Buffalo, upchucked on some unlucky soul. Off I went to Christina for some familiarity at least. A passerby grabbed my arm. A grizzled, skunk-smelling young man, and offered me the mind-altering fruits of Mother Nature: the allure of THC and onion chips. I was flattered, and if not for my present attitude, I might have indulged. Wrong as it might be.

"Christina! Christina where are you?" I yelled out to the ball of noise in the center of the living room. I can't say that Christina didn't mean a lot to me as a friend, though nothing more than that is she. This may seem like a 'Dear Diary' journal entry to you, dear reader, but I actually fear for myself. There was no one I could truly talk to in this group of people. All alone was I. How sad.

"Christina! You've made me the happiest guy on earth, I hope you know! You're beautiful and amazing and I've been just... wanting this for a long, long time," a nearby young man, or suitor, said to her. Christina was all the way across the room from me, timid me, who wouldn't have ever tried anything daring. It's my typical attitude, but I suppose things work out for the best. I mean, I suppose things for Neil Feins works out best. Somehow.

With hopes dead at the same moment they began, Christina was then crowded by Cindy, Sindy, Scindy, and Csindy (I don't actually know many of her friends. Call me an awful guy if you must.) I then decided to visit a nearby drink for a friend.

"Hey buddy," young Neil first said with gloom to his voice.

"Hennmm, I wannaugha drinngh," came the reply of a most brilliant young man (a.k.a. Kevin).

"Speak up guy!" This individual wasn't the most coherent. What I would've given to be in the place of the guy before me. I verbally and physically expressed the desire for booze, which this moronic companion of mine finally understood after repeated attempts. With a drink in my hand, I felt a part of this party. But tasting whatever was in my cup (as it was filled with liquid from a clear bottle), I felt on my tongue the full blast from a blowtorch combined with the death of many, many brain cells. The pain was so great. The pain was intense. The pain made me giggle uncontrollably like I was a young college student! Laughing and lounging were no longer mutually exclusive as I sat beside Kevin, who was no longer the moronic companion, but a highly thoughtful individual with personal goals and worries.

"I don't have anything to do! Or anything to panic about! Tonight I will be I, nothing more!" It was my optimistic translation of the following: "I dagh harbar any mpgh to drughf! Orgi ayntihgn to somke wth! Tonight, I will fublin I wanggght mresgh!" As for what state Neil Feins was in, I can't say it was stable. Is Christina still here? I asked myself, and upon seeing her I saw it was true. I did not even need to look to know that she was locking lips with some lucky gentleman of the night. Woe is me, lost and lonesome devoid of one good companion! Yet nor am I completely alone from the presence of people! Good old Kevin!

The glorious and good philosopher, with which my provoking thoughts I shared.

"Do you think? Do you ever think? Hey, I just gotta ask this dumbass question," said I. "Do you ever think that aliens are watching us?"

"Aliens would be hyper-intelligent beings if they could observe our species from the depths of space at the current moment, as that would display eons of future technology, don't you think?" Translated from: "Alien? Flubbink htae thagh more."

Kevin had weird ears. Not ears that were ever normal to any human being. By weird ears, I really mean they were melting, literally in liquid and metaphorically with the light. "Your ears," I inquired, and explained how monstrous in design they looked. I misspoke by saying they melted. The true nature of his ears appeared to be grotesque, slimy flaps that resembled the shape of a dachshund's, and then decay began. No pair of eyes besides mine noticed the skin peeling off Kevin's face, and in place of a bright eggshell skull that I expected to see, there was a series of tentacles all aligned vertically, side by side. The alignment caused pieces of a face to be put together in completion. Navy hushed lips hissed breath to my frail nostrils. The nose was two separate tentacles jutting from the face tendrils, and I felt my cheeks to garner my scent. The eyes pierced my soul the most, as two plates the size of quarters projected rays of visible light into my eyes.

"Something wrong?" it asked.

"No! No, I just— bathroom," I said with anxiety coursing through my every part.

"I'll be going now." Absent-mindedly, I did attend the restroom, which was filthy, but what could I ask from a college party? You share my sentiments, dear reader, but more importantly, why did I see what I saw? Is the marble toilet white as can be? Check. Water still cold against the feel of my cheeks? Check. Does alcohol still feel terrible against my taste buds? I looked down before sipping from my beverage, and saw an abomination! Oceanic waves with starlight rays surrounded a monstrosity, the sheer smallness of my palm! Neil Feins is not okay. . .

I am not okay. . .

Feil Neins is not okay. . .

The being housed by my red cup was disturbing, at the very least, to me. A turtle crossed with the slime of a slug, touched by the liberty of open-air, and the thing even took delight at the pain of my head, which was steadily increasing the more I looked towards the thing. It's damned jaw! The thing had holes of darkness for teeth, not simply holes in its jaw but actual black holes it seemed. My head became a Rubik's cube, breaking apart from itself with animosity. To leave it to the laymen, I was out cold. FUBAR, as they would claim.

One expects a nice change from a series of night terrors, which I secretly hoped all this was, but no. That was yet to be the case. My eyes opened after a series of voices chanting my name, wherein my tongue appeared to be wrapped in something. Was this not only the night of my first drink, but my first kiss as well? I let my eyes feast on the beautiful girl, but found a tower of ghostly pale flesh with one-two-four-eight-sixteen eyes, and rather than lips pink and sensual, there was a seventeenth eye in—down—my throat. Every other eye of this being opened up and revealed a burst of puss, black as fetid meat, followed by a tentacle with thorns I choose not to describe, as this liquid with the addition of a tentacle both went down my throat. Sorry, the succubus-monster-thing-she-beast-whatever muttered to me. My body! My insides! All were in pain and violated due to all of the aforementioned puss. My so called sign of affection concluded, leaving a taste of murky dishwater covering the wet hair of a dog on my buds. And due to the concern of my health (Am I gonna die?), I began inquiring to my friends, or nightmares. I asked if my death was coming, to which I received angry grunts which I did not entirely understand.

Love was in the air as the tentacle and black death of attraction was introduced to another. The spire of skin, with the enlarged cranium, and sixteen eyes with a seventeenth for a mouth, approached Kevin, my good chum. I must have imagined Kevin losing his head, as now before me was a normal skunk-smelling, bill-hat-wearing young man. The eye went down his throat, just as it had my violated young torso, and after a moment he was fine! He even waved to me! I raised my hand to wave back, yet before I began my gesture the man covered all sides of the room! I blinked, surprised at this, and in his place was a caterpillar of sunny and leafy strands of meat. Muscles I believe. His same face of tentacles remained; he was as I witnessed him a moment ago. Kevin, or pseudo-Kevin, crawled on many legs in a slow, sluggish manner. My head pounded the more I observed Kevin, so I had to quiet the image. Still, it burned into my mind.

Say goodbye to Christina and get out. Don't change like Kevin. Though I felt like sweat was beading on my face, and that my skin became an entity trying to crawl off my bones. I left to the bathroom, which in the present moment looked as if it were completely unaffected by the madness just outside this door of wood. I looked to the mirror, expecting the same otherworldly effects, but nothing! Just my face. My handsome, acne-ridden, greasy human face that I wouldn't change for the world. A second glance at the bathroom, my mistake it was! The hardwood floor was a living, breathing, perspiring beast of some ungodly sort! The mere touch of its skin began to melt away at my shoes, while the carpets slithered out of themselves and became clusters of slugs that were so bright my own human eyes cracked open, and felt as if they were new appendages entirely. Perhaps the most shocking, however, was looking into the mirror a second time. I couldn't tell from the feeling but I was crying, and also a being trapped between this form and the next stage! I was transparent but infinite! Scales and stars made my form. Gods extinguished with a flick of my wrist, and an exhale of breath tore the roof from this home.

Say bye to Christina.

Leave.

My objectives were set out before me, but how could I make sense of any of this chaos? I woke up with greasy skin and blood in my cheeks, to witness the Heavens and Cold ruining whatever was above our heads! Behind the creature, a void of purple and black consumed whatever celestial bodies existed in its place before. It spoke at me, claiming to Neil Feins: "Welcome to Narcelskpe."

What this was, I cannot say, as I only left the bathroom and clung to the walls. I was stumbling, my head hurt worse than anything, and I just wanted to sleep until I saw Christina! "Come here," I wave and shouted, but she only gave me a gesture to wait, as the pile of skin readied its seventeenth eye. No! I yelled and tried to reach her before I was stopped by the overbearing hand of the Heavens and Cold. It laughed and separated the house in two, with Christina in the living room side of the home. I inhabited the bathroom and hallway side of the home. The Heavens and Cold, a looming beast of dimensions and skies, swatted Christina's side of the home out of my path and out of existence. A hand neared my side of the home, and with six or twelve fingers it approached. The grasp was too much. My head pounded with fiery pain.

"I wish you didn't disturb that which was not your own creation, or that of your friend."

"I just want to leave," I pleaded.

"Exploration is just too daunting with possibilities is it not? Here you are, in a place untouched by laws natural to your world. The punishment for such a transgression to this is not light."

"Then let me go be back home," I begged.

"Not possible, unless of course, you promise to warn the others..."

"Let me leave please? I'll do anything!" I was nearly on my knees, or at least would have been if I thought of such things at the moment.

"Hear me then. Warn friend and foe alike against Eberrite if you have the slightest affection for your world and the laws of it. Thus you are warned. Relish in your moment of clarity and anguish."

I woke up. My dorm room was as awful as it once was, but I cannot recall a time it was ever good to live in. I also cannot recall how I arrived back there. I went to school, and between classes, I met the glorious Kevin, which was the very cause of a massive migraine any moment I stared too long at him. Nevertheless, Kevin gave me a beverage, for free! Kevin was telling me that it was as strong as anything else college students could acquire. The label read off as: Eberrite. Kevin then informed me about the legends of old, all claiming that drinking such a beverage reveals more to human beings than they would like to know. But it was all a myth he claimed, as he laughed it off and kept drinking. I tried a little taste, and then spoke once more.

"I think I'm done. You really shouldn't drink any more of that you know."

"Eh, fine. Your loss then my man," he said as he left.

I looked into the glass of a window and saw myself in front of a black and purple void. I was brightened by stars! My skin was slimy and cold to the touch! I blinked and was myself once more. I left for class, feeling uneasy about the stars around me. Were they really aligned in such an awful way?

Vijay Johnson-Tanco is both a freelance author and a student at University of Oregon. He has earned an award for his prowess in language arts, and has previously published his short stories "A Nice Dinner" and "The Fall of a Butterfly" in The Literary Yard, an online journal. Among his studies, he has encountered the work of H.P. Lovecraft, one of the primary influences of science fiction media and literature of the twentieth century, and has deeply admired such stories as "Dagon," "The Alchemist," and "The Mountains of Madness."

Golem

D Waggett

A WOMAN IN A SMART skirt and white blouse pushed against the door with her shoulder. It opened slowly, heavy items sliding against the floor behind it. When she had made a gap large enough, she slipped through. The sight shocked Anne. Books littered the floor. Torn pages were strewn across every surface. Glass crunched under her shoes as she walked to the old oak desk. Anne gently lifted a misshapen doll off the top, dusting off debris. She pulled it in tight to her chest.

"Wake up, Ben," she whispered. Then she raised her voice. "Come on little one, your father is probably missing you."

The doll's tiny eyes fluttered. His small hand clenched and he parted his lips Anne shook him gently and wiped her hand across his forehead. His eyes opened and blue pupils dilated slowly. Not as quick as a person would have. The figure tried to speak, his mouth working, but only squeaks came out.

"It's ok, Ben. You'll get the hang of that," she soothed. "I can't believe you actually worked. Dr. DeBuin will be ecstatic. Oh, I'm Anne."

"Anne," Ben croaked.

"Oh my God," Anne gasped. "That's it Ben. The good doctor was right. He believed that with science on his side he could get a Golem to speak and be like a normal human. It's written in legends that Golems couldn't speak, also that they had to be made by divinity, but oh well."

Anne rattled away as she strode around the room looking for items the doctor might want or need.

She opened the bottom drawer of the oak desk and pulled out a tatty leather messenger bag. Ben watched her as she moved around. He wiggled his legs, twisting his feet. They squeaked in the black leather shoes. His tan shorts were covered with tiny pieces of broken glass and stains from dried liquids. His cream jumper was missing a sleeve. It had been ripped off and was lying by the desk. Anne was busy sorting papers off the floor, bookshelves, and out of the drawers and placing them in a neat pile on the desk. She picked up a thick, dark leather journal and added it to the already bulging bag. She turned to Ben.

"I guess we need to get you some more clothes, don't we?"

Ben nodded his tiny terracotta head. The hair fell into his eyes. Anne swept it away and put him back onto the floor.

"You're so tiny. No bigger than my six-year-old nephew."

"Why?" Ben asked.

"Why what, sweetie?"

"Alone."

He wobbled on his feet. This was the first time he had ever used them. Ben held onto the table for support. When he felt stable enough he moved away gently, walking slightly duck-footed. Anne watched him, a gentle, adoring look on her face. Her brown eyes shone in the dusty midday light filtering through the torn blinds.

"I'm not sure." She felt awful. What could she say? "I don't think he would have left you without a really good reason. He never told me much about his work. About you. Only the bare essentials. He said that he was making himself a child. A golem. He was hoping that you could be what he never had. I can see he was probably right. You're amazingly human. If it wasn't for the terracotta tinge to your skin, or the slight difference in the shape of your head, you would definitely pass for a human child." Anne wiped at the mark on his face.

"Father?" Ben asked, reaching for Anne.

"I don't know where he is, but I'm hoping that his journal will tell us. I thought that he might still be here. He never said anything about leaving. How am I supposed to do my job if the doctor's not around?"

She turned a wayward chair upright and sat, pulling the journal from her bag. The twine fell away in her hands as she pulled at it gently. The cover creaked as it opened. Anne fell into silence as she read the inventor's entries. Ben watched her face. He copied her when she frowned slightly. After a few moments, he grew bored and walked over to the bookshelf by the door. He climbed over the debris and scraped his knee on a piece of broken mirror. A trickle of dark, almost brown, blood flowed into the top of his socks.

He ran his finger through it and turned to Anne. At his hoarse croak, she looked up. Her mouth formed into a silent "o" and she grabbed a piece of cloth from the inventor's table. She carefully wiped it from his leg, marveling at how realistic this little golem was. He could even bleed! The doctor truly was amazing.

The blood looked old and partially congealed, but this level of realism was astounding. Anne had never heard of anything like this before. If only the doctor was here. He could tell Ben everything. All she could do was make sure he was safe until they were reunited.

"I need to see if this journal says where your father is, okay?" She spoke to Ben gently. "I need you to be careful."

Ben nodded shortly and shuffled away to the bookshelf. He reached for the book that was the closest to him. It was old. The cover was peeling and the spine was cracked. The pages had become stained with time and the corners were so dog eared some of them had ripped off. The silver writing on the cover and spine had faded. He had to open the page to see it was a book of Grimm's fairy tales.

"Little one, I think I've found it." She looked up at him. "He's gone to his parent's farm out in the country. Gosh, he hasn't been there in over ten years. If we can find transport, like a car, it should only take four hours at the most to get there."

Anne slid the journal back into the leather shoulder bag, heaved it across her chest, and turned to face Ben, who sat looking at the Grimm's storybook. She stood, unnoticed, and watched the little figure. He sat hunched over, his small mouth shaping out the words as a child would.

"Can you read Ben?" She grimaced. "Sorry, that sounds so rude."

"I think so," Ben croaked, his voice getting clearer the more he used it.

"Wonderful."

She knelt beside him and looked at which story he was reading.

"Sleeping Beauty." Her expression became wistful. "I loved this story as a child. These fairytales are read to children by their parents."

"I remember a voice, I think."

"Was it a man's?"

"Yes."

"Dr. DeBuin must have read to you." She stood and looked down at him. "Well, I think it's time to go. I have everything packed. Let's go find some transport."

ANNE STOOD ON THE SIDE of the street, looking up and down. A car slowly approached them. It began parking, and when the engine had shut off a man stepped out. Anne rushed forward into his path.

"Excuse me sir? Will you be heading in the direction of the DeBuin farm at all?" Anne asked sweetly.

"No. I don't go that way." The suited man said in a huff as he stepped around her.

He almost walked into Ben. He looked down, and for a still moment, he just stood and stared at him with a look of disgust. The man then suddenly stepped to the side and carried on to his front door.

"Well, how rude. I think we may have to knock on some doors. I don't know if the doctor knew any of the neighbors."

Anne walked back to the houses, looking up and down the street hoping to see more people. When no one came by, she took tentative steps up the stairs of the closest neighbor's house. Holding on to Ben's hand, she knocked on the door and waited. Within a few moments, footsteps echoed down the hall and the door opened slowly.

"Hello, I'm sorry to bother you, but did you know Dr. Debuin?" Anne asked.

"Sorry, no," the man replied sharply.

"Oh, okay. I'm sorry to have bothered—"

The man had already shut the door in their faces. Ben squeezed her hand and turned to go back down the stairs. They went to the next house and knocked on the door. Some of its black paint flaked off on her hand. As they waited, Ben reached his free hand out to a plant, sitting in a terracotta pot to his left. He rubbed his tiny fingers over the leaves and leaned as far as he could to smell them. As he was running his fingers through the leaves, the door creaked open.

An old man leant against the door and glared down at Ben, and then up to Anne. She was alarmed by the cold stare. His large white eyebrows spread across his forehead and covered half of his eyes. A deep furrow had been carved into the weathered skin of his face, and his thin lips were pursed as though he had been eating lemons.

"Yes?" The man barked.

"Oh... sorry to disturb you, but did you know a Dr. DeBuin?"

"The old crackpot from next door? Yes. Why?"

"We need help getting to the DeBuin farm, and were wondering if you could help."

"I don't go that far out. If I can help it. Is that boy okay?" The old man asked, glaring at Ben.

Anne looked down at Ben. He seemed fine. He was looking at the old man with big blue eyes, his tiny hand still in the shrub.

"Yes, Ben's fine," Anne replied slowly. She was suddenly very cautious.

"Is he the doctor's boy?" the man croaked, sneering down at the Golem. "He's funny-looking."

"Again sorry for disturbing you," Anne replied sharply. "We'll be off then."

Anne pulled Ben up into her arms. She protectively put her hand around his head and stroked his soft brown hair. Ben rested his head on her shoulder and watched the man's bent back retreat into the house. The door slammed, the sound echoing down the empty street.

"What a rude man." Anne couldn't suppress her irritation. "There is nothing wrong with you sweetheart, never let anyone tell you there is. We're all made in different shapes and sizes. The doctor made you look so much like his wife. The same colored hair. Even the same nose. But you have his eyes."

Ben rested his hands around the back of her neck, fingers entwining slightly in Anne's blonde hair. He shuffled his little body around and then settled with his head against her shoulder. She stroked at his hair and let her mind wander to the Golem's predicament. Why had the doctor left him behind? Did he not want Ben? What could have happened to him?

"Come on Ben, we should carry on. Hopefully someone will help. I can't believe more of his neighbors didn't know him," Anne huffed.

Anne shifted Ben onto her other shoulder and walked across the street to the house directly in front of the doctor's. The door's blue paint looked freshly done. The steps were clean and looked as though they were regularly swept. A brass knocker shone brightly in the afternoon sun. She knocked and took a step back.

An elderly woman answered the door. She came out onto the step. Her pale green eyes glistened in the sun, and she smiled at them sweetly.

"Can I help you, my dears?" she asked as sweetly as she smiled.

"Yes. I was hoping that maybe you knew Dr. DeBuin and his family's farm?" Anne mumbled warily.

"Of course I do. David was a childhood friend of mine. Do come on in."

Anne felt Ben shift in her arms. He had turned himself to face the pavement. Rain started to fall and the street became darker, dot by dot, until the whole street was a dark wet grey. He was fascinated and stuck his tiny hand out to catch the falling rain. As it landed it turned his terracotta skin a more vibrant red. With the fingers of his left hand, he rubbed the moisture until it became fully absorbed. He tried to catch more, but Anne had walked into the house.

The neighbor closed the door behind her and followed them down the hallway to the kitchen. The house smelled of baking bread and fresh flowers. It was warm and light, with cream walls printed with tiny blue flowers. In the center of the kitchen was a small circular oak table that looked freshly cleaned and well-loved. The rain fell heavier. The sky turned a dappled grey as though the sun was still trying to breakthrough. Ben watched. He appeared enraptured by the new sight. Anne put him onto one of the three chairs around the table so that he could continue to look through the window. The elderly woman took another and motioned for Anne to do the same.

"Are you looking for David?"

"Yes. I'm hoping to return to him." She waved a hand toward Ben. "I went on a short holiday to see my parents, came back and he was no longer there. His place is an absolute mess. It looks as though it's been ransacked by someone looking for something. The doctor was unorganized, but not that bad. I'm worried."

"I understand, dear." The old lady sighed and leant against the kitchen counter. "I'm Cara."

"Oh, I'm sorry. Anne, and this is Ben." She motioned to herself and Ben hurriedly.

"My goodness." Cara gasped, turning to Ben. "He managed to make you then. David always spoke of making a boy... Golems, I think he called them. You are so life-like, I never would have guessed."

"You knew Dr. Debuin well then?" Anne asked.

Cara disappeared into the next room. Within a minute she returned carrying a large leather-bound album. She set it carefully on the table and pushed it towards Ben, a tender smile on her sun-weathered face. She retrieved plates, forks, a knife, and a sponge cake. Then she filled the kettle and put it on the stove.

"Can't reminisce without tea and cake. The rain won't stop for a little while."

Cara eased herself carefully back into the chair and offered a slice to everyone. After wiping her hands on her yellow and blue flowered apron, she opened the album. The first picture was of a chubby smiling baby with curling hair and sparkling eyes. It was an old sepia-tone image. The picture was grainy and stained around the edges. Underneath, scrawling hand-writing read: "Cara, 14 months old"

"Me, as a tiny little thing," she mused. "Can't believe I was so cute. Wish my hair had stayed that curly though." Cara pushed her fingers into her loose, gray bun.

She turned a few more pages and then stopped at a picture of her younger self with a group of three others. The writing underneath was neater than the first, it read: "Me with David, Sarah, and John". Sarah had waist-length brown hair and was wearing a high collared white shirt. She was smiling affectionately at a young man. The man's hair was dark blonde. He wore a black jacket and suit trousers, and he was laughing with a man who wore just a plain white shirt and dark trousers. It looked as though they were having a picnic. A large wicker basket was just visible behind the two men, and they all sat on a checkered cloth.

"This was the last day that we all got to sit there as friends." Cara sounded sad. "The next day I was married to John, and the weekend after it was Sarah and David's wedding. Jobs and children came in the way of having quiet picnics after that. David was always working. He was a great scientist. My John was a lawyer, and your mother was the best seamstress around." She made three cups of tea.

Cara looked distant and slightly sad. She turned the page to another photo of David, standing in a garden that looked similar to the one outside the kitchen window. He was younger than in the previous photograph. He wore a simple white, long-sleeved shirt, black trousers and a jacket slung over his left arm. He was smiling at the camera. Ben placed his tiny fingers over the picture.

"As I said, I knew David from our childhood. We grew up together. His parents lived next door to us. We were both only children and so played together. It was like having a brother. As we got older everyone thought we would be sweethearts, but I thought of him only as a sibling. We went off to school, where I met Sarah who I introduced to David, and through him, I met John. It was always the four of us.

"From what John used to say, David always had his nose in a book about mythology. Apparently, ever since he read Pinocchio he was fascinated by Golems. Read all he could he about them. David thought maybe with the more modern science he could create one that surpassed those he had read about. And he did because here you are little one."

"It doesn't sound like he has changed much then," Anne mused. "He still does nothing but read and work on his experiments. He finally gave in and got an assistant about three years ago. Me. I never knew what he was working on though. I mainly just made sure he ate and looked after his wife when he stayed in his study. I sometimes checked his papers for him." She sighed with recollection. "She passed away a little over a year ago. After she passed, he just locked himself away. I would leave his food outside the door for him and do his shopping. I felt more like a housekeeper than an assistant.

"I guess he must have been working non-stop on you Ben." Anne turned to the golem, who was flipping through the photo album. "I sound like I'm moaning about my job, but I wouldn't have changed it for the world. The doctor was amazing, and his wife was so kind. He made the best stew you could imagine. I adored them both. I do hope he is alright. He just left so suddenly. Do you know why, Cara?"

"I have my ideas." Cara sounded more certain than she let on. "From what I heard, he was supposed to have been working on weapons for the war. But he hated it. Stopped turning up for work. Then one day I saw him get in his car and drive off. That was the last I saw of him. That must have been at least a month ago. One thing I can't understand now though is... why would he leave you behind, Ben?"

Cara piled up the plates, placed the forks on top, and put them into the sink. As she sat back down, she glanced at the window. The rain still fell, but the sky was now a pale grey and the rain was nothing more than a drizzle.

"We can probably leave soon, the rain seems to be letting up," Cara said.

"That's great. I really want to return Ben to him."

Ben turned his body to look out the window behind him. He turned back and looked at Anne, her hair tied neatly into a low ponytail, a crisp white shirt, and a dark wool skirt. Then he turned to look at Cara, her hair tied up into a loose bun, strands falling over her soft green eyes, the wrinkles making her face softer and more gentle. Both of them had kind faces and yet were so different. Ben wondered if he would change with age too, or would he always look as he did?

THE RAIN FINALLY STOPPED and the clouds turned back to a soft grey. The sky poked through a pale periwinkle blue. Cara and Anne were still flipping through the photo album that lay open on the dining table. Ben rested his head on his arms and looked at the birds that flew past the kitchen window.

"Rain gone," Ben squeaked, his voice almost sounding like a normal child's.

"Has it?" Cara asked. "Well, I guess we can head off now then. Don't want to get there too late."

She walked over to a cupboard under the sink and pulled out a wicker picnic basket. It looked almost like the one from the photograph. The wicker was paler, and this basket had a red ribbon tied onto one of the handles. She wrapped sandwiches, the remainder of the cake, and made a flask of tea and added them all to the basket.

"For the journey, little one," she had said to Ben as she gently dropped the basket onto the countertop by the door. She picked up her car keys from the key hook and motioned for Anne and Ben to walk ahead of her out of the door. Cara pointed toward the garage and headed to unlock the car doors.

"I'm afraid I don't have a child's car seat," Cara confessed. "Will he be alright, do you think?"

"I'm sure he will," Anne said.

Anne picked up the golem and placed him in the back seat of the old black car. She pulled the seatbelt over his chest and buckled him in, then checked to make sure the strap was tight. Cara slotted the picnic basket behind the driver's seat. She then slowly lowered herself behind the wheel of the car, checked that everyone was buckled in, and drove out of the garage.

THE SKY FLYING PAST the window darkened as the afternoon slowly drove onwards to evening. Anne looked through the mirror at Ben, who watched the clouds drift by. She joined him in watching them. Most of them looked like fluffy white things that had no shape, but others looked like cars or a bone. One even looked like an ice cream cone, with a huge swirling top.

"Look Ben, an ice cream cone." Anne pointed and chuckled. "You'll have to try one someday. They're so good."

The Golem's stomach began to grumble. Ben placed his tiny little hands over his rumbling belly, a look of worry on his face. Anne turned in her seat as he squirmed in the back seat. She could hear the leather creaking as he shifted.

"Are you okay, Ben?" Anne asked.

Ben rubbed his tummy. His mouth felt dry and he could only squeak when he parted his lips.

"Are you hungry, little one?" Cara asked, glancing in the rearview mirror. "There's food in the hamper. Can you reach?"

Ben struggled to reach the hamper but his small arms couldn't reach. His tiny fingers just barely touched the closest corner to him and scraped against the surface. Anne stretched behind the driver's seat and managed to grab hold of the edge of the basket. She pulled it forward enough so that Ben could reach the handle. Together they managed to push and pull it up onto the seat next to him. Ben fumbled with the old latch and opened the hamper to reveal the clear wrapped sandwiches.

After the sandwiches and the remainder of the cake were finished, and the tea gone, Ben was beginning to feel sleepy. He was comfortably full and warm. The motion of the car was soothing, and the muted chatter of Anne and Cara became like a lullaby for the golem. His eyes drooped as he rested his head against the cold glass of the window. He watched the clouds float by until he could no longer stay awake. His hands fell limply into his lap, alerting Anne.

Anne smiled when she saw that he had fallen to sleep.

"It's been a long first day for him," she said.

"Aww, poor little thing. It is weird to think that David succeeded. Something so impossible, yet there he lies looking just like a child."

"I do have to wonder why he left Ben behind, though," Anne mused.

"Honey, I have no idea. The David I knew would never leave a little thing like that behind."

"From what I've read in the journal, Dr. DeBuin has been working on Ben for over fifteen years, but it only mentions how to make one." Anne mused, pulling out the journal. "There are speculations, theories, and sketches from other books about Golems. Some lines say a full moon is needed, others that a total lunar eclipse is. You don't think that maybe he thought Ben hadn't worked and left him when he had to leave?"

"Oh no. I think that maybe he was forced out of his house by his old bosses or colleagues and didn't have time," Cara speculated. "David was attached to his journals when he was using them. If he could have, he would have packed up that book, the boy, and the photos of his wife. Were they still in the house?"

Anne thought for a moment, thinking back to what had been left in the house.

"Yes. They were on the floor. I should have thought of that and brought them with me. Do you think he'll be mad that I didn't?"

"No my dear, I don't. You're bringing him his boy. That is probably the best thing you could have ever done. He'll be over the moon."

The road began to clear of cars the closer they drove to the farm. After two and half hours, they were the only car left on the road. Occasionally they would pass by a tractor.

"Are you okay driving all the way there?" Anne asked.

"Oh how sweet of you Anne, but I can manage. I have always enjoyed driving. As soon as I learned how to drive, I did. Almost non-stop to begin with. I drove everywhere," Cara chuckled.

"Wow, it gets really dark out here," Anne stated, peering at the dark road ahead of them.

The sky was a deep blue. The sun had long set behind them and the moon was now beginning to rise. The road ahead faded into an inky nothingness beyond the car's headlights.

"It sure does. We're not too far away from the farm now. About another thirty minutes," Cara muttered.

Anne shifted in her seat and turned to look at Ben. He was still fast asleep with his head against the door. His left hand was curled around his seatbelt, holding it under his head. His other hand was draped over the hamper next to him. Cara shuffled her position slightly, trying to pull herself up into a slightly different pose.

"You really should let me drive for a while," Anne insisted. "If your back isn't stiff, I need to know your secret, 'cause mine feels like it's carved of wood."

"It's fine," Cara said. "But I'm definitely not as young as I used to be."

Finally, the lights and silhouette of a building appeared on their left. Cara turned on to the drive and proceeded slowly up the pot-holed road. The bouncing of the car jolted Ben awake. He turned bleary eyes to the sky, and his shock at how dark it had gotten showed in his rounded mouth. He turned to look at the building in front of them. In the fading light, the house looked dark blue, its cream shuttered windows almost grey. It was a two-story building with a wrap-around porch, and fields stretched off behind it.

A dark figure disappeared behind a twitching curtain. The porch light switched on and the door opened. A man stepped out, the light behind him blotting out any features. Cara stepped out of the car first as Anne pulled Ben out of the back seat.

"Who is it?" came the deep gruff voice of the shadowy figure.

"David? It's me, Cara," Cara answered uncertainly.

"Cara? What are you doing here so late? I wasn't expecting you was I?"

Anne stepped up to the side of Cara, Ben held safely in her arms. When she stepped into the light David looked shocked to see her. Then his eyes fell onto the tiny figure.

"Dr. DeBuin," Anne sighed in relief. "I'm so glad I found you."

The doctor's eyes never left Ben. He tentatively stepped forward, then stopped when Ben turned his head to look back at him. He was frozen by those blue eyes so like his own. Anne shifted Ben slightly and walked towards the doctor, Cara close behind.

"Doctor, meet Ben. Ben this is your father, for lack of a kinder term," Anne said gently, looking softly at the Inventor.

"He worked. I... I just left... When did you find him?" the Dr. stuttered.

"This morning," Anne replied. "I went looking for you. He was asleep where you left him."

"David. Rude," Cara admonished. "Let your weary guests in please."

"Oh my goodness, of course. Please come in."

Cara stepped into the hallway first, Anne walked behind her and David trailed behind. He closed the door, never taking his eyes from Ben. A look of shock etched onto the pale wrinkled flesh. His mouth hung open slightly and he kept running his hands through his wavy grey hair.

Cara led them all along the hallway and into the living room. She sat down in an overstuffed cream armchair. Anne moved over to the sofa and gently placed Ben onto the soft, mismatched cushions. Ben looked around him at the photos that lined the magnolia-painted walls. He turned his head to take in the old television set in the corner, the white net curtains, the dark wood bookshelves and matching table.

His legs were stretched out in front of him and he looked like a doll. His shorts were wrinkled and stained with jam, and his jumper had flour streaked down the front. Anne wiped at a stain on his cheek. She wasn't sure what it was or even what it had been. She also wiped down his sweater and swept his hair to the side, trying to make him seem more presentable.

"Why did you... leave me?" Ben asked, sadness in his tone and eyes.

"Oh Ben, I—" The doctor shifted his weight, rubbed his arm and dropped his gaze to the floor. "I had to. That sounds like such a pathetic excuse, but it's true. I was sure you hadn't worked." David sighed.

He moved closer to Ben and tentatively sat next to his creation, always watching. The doctor brushed his hand through Ben's hair. "It feels so real. Your skin is as warm and soft as a human." He breathed in shock and pulled Ben onto his knee.

"I just—I can't believe you worked. I can't process this, it's so unbelievable. You're here. My son is here." The doctor breathed in ecstasy.

"But why?" Ben asked again.

"Oh yes, sorry, I'm just so happy to see you." The doctor said hurriedly. "I thought you hadn't worked. I got a phone call from a colleague I once worked with. His bosses were planning on raiding the house. They thought I had information on an experiment we worked on over fifteen years ago. I didn't, not that they believed me. I left and came here, no one knew about this place."

"I knew," Cara interrupted.

"I know that, Cara. But none of my colleagues did. I didn't even have time to pack anything up. My friend called just as they were leaving, within half an hour they would have turned up."

"What were you working on?" Anne asked.

"Weapons of war, something I am not proud of. It's why I left them."

Anne looked shocked. "I never knew. I never thought you were that kind of scientist."

"Oh Anne, I know. But as I said, it's why I left. I couldn't stomach it, but I guess they thought I knew too much or I had other information. I took what money I had saved and locked myself away."

"You always did have a strong moral compass, David," Clara chimed. The doctor smiled.

"I'll go put on some tea for everyone," Cara added.

"Kettle's not long been boiled," the doctor said to Cara as she passed him.

"We were all wondering, though, why they left Ben completely untouched," Anne asked turning to look at Ben. "Did they not know about him?"

The doctor looked thoughtful. "Maybe they thought he was just a doll. I never told anyone about my interest in Golems. I remembered how everyone thought I was weird in school."

"Here's the tea," Cara offered the tray to each person.

"When I was a boy, my father read Pinocchio to me," the doctor explained. "I guess that sparked it all off. After that, I researched Golems and found out as much as I could from the books available to me. Most of it was very religious and all about the magic of it. I did manage to find some that talked about making Golems in a scientific manner."

"Why would you make... a Golem?" asked Ben, pointing to himself.

"I grew up reading stories about making Golems. As a child, I wanted to make one as a brother for myself. Obviously none of them worked. I went to school. I grew up. I met my wife and we tried for years to have children. Nothing worked." He sighed looking down at his hands. "We gave up trying the natural way and I managed to convince Sarah that we could make a Golem."

He paused, took a sip of his tea, and looked at his creation. "It took a long time to make you. I went through so much clay. I'm a perfectionist," David chuckled. "I wanted you to look just as we imagined. My wife drew an image of you once, she decided we should try to equally combine our looks to make you. Her hair, my eyes. I tried to make you look more like her though. She was my angel."

David sighed and glanced at the wall. At the photos of Sarah.

"She wanted me too?" Ben squeaked in a tiny voice.

The two women sat enraptured in the recounting. Cara brought her teacup to her lips, only to realize it was empty. Instead, she placed it on the table. Anne had turned to face the doctor and Ben. Her own tea was untouched and cold. Occasionally, she would brush Ben's hair or pet his knee.

"Of course she did," the doctor said. "We both wanted you so badly. Unfortunately, Sarah got a chest infection and it progressed into pneumonia. She became bedridden for the last two years of her life, then passed away. My heart was broken." He paused. "I just threw myself into making you. For her." David hesitated. "I hired Anne in those last few years, to help with Sarah's constant care and the house, I couldn't cope with it alone. She became my assistant and helped with re-organizing my papers, bringing me food. She would even read through my papers for spelling mistakes. God knows I made a few."

"I barely understood any of his papers," Anne teased. "I had to look up the very long scientific words to make sure they were right."

"You did great, Anne," the doctor reassured her. "I could not have managed without you." His attention turned to Ben, taking in his creation. "I left the house about a month before you woke up. I feel so stupid. It must have been the lunar eclipse. As stupid as this may sound, maybe a little bit of magic was needed. In the words of J.M.Barrie, the writer of Peter Pan—I can't wait to read that to you—'All you need is faith, trust, and pixie dust.' I guess he was sort of right. Science could only get me so far, but I guess I needed the universe to help with the rest, and answer my prayers."

The doctor suddenly moved to stand. "I think, because it's so late, we should all go to bed. Cara, Anne, I think it best if you stayed the night. I can't have two ladies driving back all that way at this hour."

"I think that is for the best David," Cara sighed with a yawn.

She pushed herself out of the chair and headed to her car, retrieving an old suitcase before slamming the trunk shut. Dragging the battered case back into the house, she was met by a smirking David and a stunned Anne.

"You never know when you have to spend the night somewhere," she said matter-of-factly.

"That's true," David chuckled, as if he had expected nothing less. "I have spare toiletries upstairs in the bathroom if you need them Anne. Also I think some of Sarah's clothes will fit you."

"That will be greatly appreciated doctor," Anne said, headed toward the stairs. She paused before going up. "Oh, I forgot. I brought some of your things from home. Your journal and some of your papers. But I didn't think to bring your photos."

"It's okay, I have copies." Still, there was sadness in his eyes. "Instead you have brought me something so much more important. My son. The journal is nothing more than paper now he has worked."

"Do you need help with your suitcase, Cara?" the doctor asked.

"No thanks, I'm not completely infirm."

Cara lugged her suitcase up the stairs and took the largest spare room. Anne said goodnight to everyone and went into the room beside Ben's. Dr. DeBuin picked up an exhausted Ben and carried him into the smallest room. Its walls were painted white and blue, reminiscent of a nautical theme with a lighthouse lamp and well-loved model ships on the clean shelves.

"This used to be my room when I was a very young boy, before we moved to the city," the doctor told Ben. "I have so much to teach you. That can all wait though. I'm so truly happy that you're here. I'm so happy. I have my son. Sarah would adore you."

The doctor helped Ben into soft, clean pajamas, taught him how to brush his teeth—which Ben managed very messily—combed his hair, and tucked him into the plush bed. He pulled up the covers to Ben's chin, gave him a teddy bear, and kissed him on the forehead. As he walked out of the room, he turned to look at the child he never thought would exist, smiled, and walked into his own room. The lights all went off one by one and the house fell into a content silence.

D Waggett writes science fiction, mainly aiming at the young adult genre. She is currently working on a novel concept for NaNoWriMo and short story pieces to submit online. She enjoys writing and illustrating fairy tale retellings. Her main inspirations come from Terry Pratchett, J.K. Rowling, and Tolkein. She currently lives in Tamworth with her husband and cat, who thinks it's a dragon and hates net curtains. She also works for the local council in the tourist information center.

Sleeper

Chris Keaton

STAN WAS A FAT MAN and everyone knew it. He knew it. His wife knew it but didn't complain. His coworkers knew it and showed him that they knew with their snickers and sidelong looks. Jerry, his boss, knew it and reminded him constantly of it: "Stan, beauty sells."

Jerry was right. In the world of pharmaceutical sales, he was an anomaly. Jerry, and hell, all of Stan's coworkers, looked like they stepped out of a fashion magazine. He knew his high sales rate was the only thing keeping him employed. But no matter how much he sold, the snide comments didn't stop.

Stan was feeling all of his 270 pounds as he wrestled his suitcase up the stairs to his third-floor hotel room. What kind of hotel takes their one elevator offline for maintenance? Stan knew Jerry booked him in this shithole just to take another little stab at the fat man.

The Jaws theme blasted from his pants pocket. Stan took the phone call as a chance to have a breather on the second-floor landing. Maybe it's time to do something about my weight. Through his heavy breaths, he caught a faint whiff of urine. Damn, he thought, this place is a dump.

Jaws was insistent. Stan checked the phone and the caller ID read CALLER OUT OF RANGE. Being winded and not thinking straight, Stan didn't wonder why he'd never seen a message like that before. He was just happy for an interruption from his embarrassing climb.

He lifted the phone to his ear and was met with a brain-splitting screech of buzzes and beeps he vaguely recognized as an old modem or fax machine when you dialed the wrong number.

Stan jerked the phone from his ear. "Son of a bitch!" he exclaimed a little louder than he'd wanted.

He stuffed the phone in his pocket and finished the rest of his climb without having a heart attack. He was sweating and panting like he'd run a marathon by the time he reached his room. That's when he got the second call. Stan fumbled with the room key and the phone. He wanted to get into the room as fast as he could, since he was sweating in a most undignified way. If no one spotted him sweating, he wouldn't need to address it. At least that's what he told himself. He took a deep breath and was set to give a calm greeting when he was hit with the screeching buzzes and beeps. Stan jumped and shouted, "Shit!" He nearly dropped his phone in the process.

After he threw the three deadbolts into place, Stan rubbed his temples in an attempt to reduce the throb in his head. Stan gave the room a disgusted once over. There are no locks against the bed bugs I'll probably bring home. He kicked the covers off the one bed and sat down. His head was killing him and the wrong number hadn't helped.

His phone rang again.

Stan flopped back on the bed and held the phone a few inches from his ear before he answered, just to be on the safe side. He was met with a cheery woman's voice. Stan put the phone against his ear and answered properly: "Hello."

"Hello, Stan?"

She may not have aged well, but neither has he. However, through it all, she was the only constant light in his life, and he always smiled when he heard her voice. "Yes, hon."

"How are you?" He knew she honestly wanted to know.

"Besides a splitting headache, I'm good. The demo went well."

"I knew you'd do it." She said with obvious honesty. "Jerry will have to give you the lead on the next release."

Stan frowned because he knew that wasn't going to happen. The next release was a prescription weight loss pill, and in the words of Jerry, "It doesn't look good to have a fat man sell a diet pill."

"Yeah, sure," Stan answered with little cheer.

"Well, you just sound terrible. It's late. Get some sleep. I'll see you tomorrow."

Stan smiled again. "Yes, I love you."

"Oh, and when you get home, I think there may be something wrong with the power. It's been cutting in and out. Really weird."

"Okay, I'll check it out."

"I love you, Stan"

Stan said his goodbye and ended the call. He laid there a moment and contemplated whether he wanted to take his clothes off or just go to sleep where he lay. Falling asleep on the spot was going to win over when the phone rang again.

"So, what'd you forget?" Stan answered, expecting his wife. But when the screeching buzzes and beeps hit him, he threw the phone across the room.

"Damn it," he muttered as he picked the pieces of his phone off of the floor. Stan tried to puzzle the pieces back together, but it was toast, so he dropped the remains in the trash. He rubbed his bloodshot eyes and raided the mini-fridge, pouring a couple of bottles of cheap whiskey into a hotel glass that he washed twice, just to be safe.

Stan sipped on the drink as the room's phone rang. He wanted to just let it ring, but maybe they were going to alert him to a huge booking mistake and upgrade him to their El Presidente Suite, as if they had one. He chuckled at the thought when he answered. Stan was slammed by the same buzzes and beeps he'd been getting all night. He pulled the phone away from his ear and shouted at it, "What the fuck do you want?

Leave me alone!" He slammed the receiver down. My head isn't a damned computer.

He scrambled into his bag and found a packet of aspirin. Stan washed them down with the last bit of his whiskey.

The room phone rang again.

Stan stared at the phone, willing it to explode. But all it did was ring. He lifted the receiver and didn't hear anything. Slowly, cautiously, he brought the receiver up to his ear. Still nothing.

"Hello?"

The buzzes and beeps screamed out at him.

In a fit of rage, Stan tore the phone from the dresser and threw it across the room. "Bill me, assholes."

Stan opted to take off only his shirt and pants. As little contact with the sheets as possible was his preferred strategy. Beyond that, his throbbing head didn't allow for much thought. He flicked on the TV and was met with a news report complaining about power outages and cell phone problems, which the bubbly news reporter attributed to solar flares. Stan didn't follow much of it because he was fast asleep in seconds.

Soon the television dropped into static, but this did little to disturb Stan's comatose-like sleep. It only lasted a few minutes before jumbled images of planets, machines, and anatomy replaced the static, which was almost immediately accompanied by the same screeching beeps and buzzes that had haunted Stan over the phone.

Stan stirred as if in a nightmare. Sweat beaded on his forehead, but he soon settled back down under the buzzes and screeches coming from the television.

Several hours later, Stan awoke from his sleep with the television quiet. He felt oddly refreshed ready to take on the new day. He just couldn't put his finger on what he was supposed to be doing. Every time he tried the thought slipped away like Jell-O through his fingers. The thought made him smile. The thought of Jell-O didn't come from a desire for it—he loathed Jell-O—but he wasn't hungry at all. He'd never woke up not hungry. He'd think about this later. Right now, he needed to shower and seize the day.

Stan stood and went to open the curtains to let in the early morning sunrise. That was what he planned to do, anyway. But what he did do was grab the curtains as a body wide muscle cramp threw him to the ground, which took the curtain and rod with him. He screamed out. Stan knew the entire hotel had to have heard him, but he didn't care. This pain was the worst he'd ever felt, even topping his kidney stone by three. Was this a heart attack?

Stan managed to get himself up onto all fours. There was a bloodstain on the rug that he was pretty sure wasn't there a minute ago. "Oh that's nasty." A drop of blood fell from his face, adding to the stain. He reached up and touched his face. His hand came away with a hunk of flesh. Panic set in as he rushed, as fast as the pain would allow him, into the dingy bathroom. "The hell is happening?"

Stan stood in front of the mirror under the yellowy bathroom light. The flesh that had fallen off belonged to a portion of his right cheek. With no thought or reason or pain, Stan dug his finger into the wound. He easily tore the flesh away, revealing something hard and black underneath.

"Oh, my God... mmvee tt..." Stan's speech was replaced with an insect-like buzz.

Stan's mission to rid himself of the rotting flesh continued unabated. Hunks of hair attached to flesh splattered onto the soiled tile floor. His bloody shirt—along with most of his chest—fell next, landing with a sickening slap. It went on like this until all that remained was the New Stan.

The generations that he had waited for that call disappeared in the instant when he remembered he was, in English, Invasion Unit 34196, and his sole purpose in life was to secure this sector for the arrival of the terra-formers.

This new Stan was no longer unsure of himself. He admired his new smooth, polished black head devoid of features. His new head joined a strong neck, which connected to a solid torso plated with the same polished black material. He flexed his newly powerful mecha-biological arms. Invasion Unit 34196 was satisfied that his host unit achieved optimum body mass facilitating conversion.

The buzz and beep of his command unit called to him from the primitive video display unit in the other room. He marched into the room and took his commands from the television. Invasion Unit 34196 spared a momentary glance outside the window at the burning city. All in all, he was satisfied with the invasion's progress.

He stepped into the hallway and neutralized two bi-pedal hominids. As he stepped over their remains, he thought:

Stan was a good soldier and everyone will soon know it.

Chris Keaton is an Air Force veteran living with his family in sunny Arizona. He has produced several short films and currently has a thriller in production. But filmmaking isn't his only passion. He has recently started to whet his appetite for telling stories by writing prose. He also has a book undergoing final edits.

Eclipsed

Jasmine Yuen-Carrucan

THE CHILDREN'S GIGGLES LIFTED and bounced across the enormous curved panelling of the planetarium. The class of six-year-olds raised their hands to receive the solar eclipse safe goggles from Sarah.

"There isn't much time," she said, placing the last pair of chunky tinted plastic in the soft fingers of the last child, Emily, "and if you don't have these on, you don't look up."

The class teacher, Miss Beasel, helped each child make sure the goggles were fit and fastened. Sarah looked down at the sparkling girl next to her, determined to manage everything alone. "Shall I help you with that Emily?" The girl's cheeks flushed, half embarrassed, half proud that her mother, the most qualified astrophysicist in the building, was bending over to help her.

"In about ten minutes our moon will pass between the earth and the sun, and we'll be lucky enough to be standing in the shadow. Who's ready?"

The children squealed and cheered their best response as Sarah and Miss Beasel ushered them outside onto a viewing balcony already packed with onlookers. The air was festive. Adults clipped photos of each other in their eclipse sunnies, phones were occupied as viewpoints across the city were compared, and jobs paused. This moment in history demanded time. It was a momentary free pass from all the norms. The children, still excited, pressed into a tighter circle, protectively shepherded by Miss Beasel and Sarah whose eyes stretched up and skyward.

Sarah felt Emily's hand timidly slip into her own. Mother and daughter exchanged a look, with more feeling than seeing from behind their protective glasses. This moment shared between them would not happen again, not in their lifetime anyway. Sarah wished to feel the even lighter pressure of little Jake on her other hand, her balance somewhat off without both children by her side. Her thoughts flashed to the face of the three-year-old boy, his kindergarten play oblivious to the great shadow about to pass above them. She hoped he was inside, that he wouldn't feel her looking skyward and suddenly search for a window. Sarah squeezed Emily's hand as her voice went out to the children.

"Okay boys and girls, here we go."

Countless pairs of protected eyes looked toward the heavens as the shadow slid across their skin. The dogs stopped barking first; the bugs and birds fell silent; then the electric hum of the world went with it. The shadowed disc through Sarah's glasses looked just like it was supposed to, just as the textbooks described.

The fidgeting started. The children first, shuffling their little feet. The trick of time, Sarah thought, the minute that seems like an hour lost contact with measure.

From a few feet away came a statement of civilised bewilderment: "My phone's stopped working"; and rising from the other end of the balcony: "Hey, what happened to my phone?"

Excitement shifted to angst and the children sucked in the air of disruption. Miss Beasel jabbed at the phone in her hand, trying to wake it up.

"Mummy?"

Sarah's eyes were on her own phone, its lifeless black reflecting only her frowning, goggle-clad look. She turned to see the fear on her daughter's face.

The push of the crowd forced them inside. A security guard threw protective arms around Miss Beasel and the children while Sarah searched beyond the room for answers. As the cloud of confusion swirled, she took Emily in her arms. No phones—mobile or landline—no electricity, and the shadow of the eclipse remained. This was not in the textbooks.

Her first thought was Jake, and as they reached the front of the building this thought turned to panic. The front sliding doors were smashed, the final cry of their failure to release the questioning masses. The two blocks to Jake's kindergarten collapsed beneath the command of a new chaos. Cars jammed the streets, people scattered the paths, and the grey shadow of the eclipse remained.

"Don't let the children out and don't look at the sun," was the brief she gave the remaining carers at the kindergarten as she secured her own goggles across young Jake's eyes. He was scared but happy to see them, the distinction between excitement and fear hard for the three-year-old to make.

"Can we go home?" he asked. And without voice, Sarah asked herself the exact same question: Can we?

The trains were down. The buses were overthrown and occupied by desperate adults with no mind for children. The forty-minute car ride home would be impossible, at least for now. Sarah's office at the Planetarium was their only option.

Inside, the building was quiet, all posts now deserted. Mother and children moved quickly through the cafeteria. Plastic wrapped food crinkled under Sarah's fingertips as she filled a garbage bag with as much food as was manageable. She would pay the people back; she'd promised the children whose eyes had bulged at the sight of the stealing. She would pay them back.

Up the stairs, across the far east wing, Sarah closed the double door to the hallway first, then locked and blocked it with a large table and filing cabinet. Adrenaline powered remote control moved her to make order out of chaos as she dashed about the offices collecting waste paper baskets, cups, and vases. Jake supervised the water filling, and Emily struggled to carry the slurping containers to Sarah's office. Small and large hands dragged all supplies through the final door. Sarah secured the room, locking the door and massing a mountain of heavy furniture behind it. For a moment she considered her actions as overreactions, imagining an hour from now when the lights would flicker on and her colleagues would discover the crazy digs she'd built for herself and the children. The moment passed and Sarah kept on.

Real darkness took the place of the solar eclipse shadow. Makeshift beds were formed from jackets, coats, and towels, and Sarah held the two small bodies of Emily and Jake until they found a sleeping peace from the outside grumbling. The children had asked often about Chris. When would they see their father? How would he find them? It would take time, she'd said, but he'd find them. How indeed? The web of texts, emails, and video chats they'd spun to keep the family together under the guise of globalisation had suddenly dissolved. How would Chris manage to cross the five thousand kilometres that now separated them? She looked at her phone for the thousandth time, hoping to see a sign of digital life. There was none.

Sarah waited for the sun to rise, but it never came. Shades of black turned grey and with the return of that lifeless hue, the world outside lost itself in the chaos of panic.

In their refuge, they played games, crafted, and talked. As always the children made the best of the worst. There was the hope it would end. That everything would turn itself back on. Everything would right its wrong.

One day turned to two; two to three. From the street, the square blanketed window of their cave lay anonymous. When the first cries for help rang in from the street below, Emily and Jake expected an explanation. After the fourth or fifth, the children stopped asking but their bodies failed never to flinch.

Gunfire began on day two, as did the sometimes swirling choppers overhead. It would be days until the world woke fully to its new self. The shadow of the eclipse would not cover the entire planet, but the strength of its curse could. All digital fields were destroyed, scrambled beyond repair, the travel of power stumped, leaving the world scurrying for any turn of fuel-filled motor. Billions of dollars were sucked swiftly into an electronic void—stocks, credits, and debts all slopped to nothing. The rich were suddenly poor and the poor were suddenly equal to the rich. The city bore the heart of the decay. Looting began quickly, and mounting unstoppable violence raged with it.

This was no place for children.

Sarah kept them away from the window. The fourth-floor view was high enough to be safe from the crowd but low enough to sense the color of the violence. No one had come to their door. Not yet. But Sarah knew they would, she knew their time was limited.

On the fourth day, the fires began. Black burning smoke crept into their window, smelling sometimes sweet and sometimes sickly, its first heavy scent reminding Emily, strangely, of fairy floss.

They took what they could, moving quietly and quickly in a single unit down the fire stairs toward the underground car park. Sarah wished she wasn't alone, that strength and decisions could be sourced from someone else, but all options stopped at her. She squeezed Emily's hand and led them forward. A gunshot blew on the street outside and Jake clung tighter to her neck, burying his quivering breath beneath her ear. Their fear created the knot that would hold them to any end. Together.

The last door in the stairway echoed open, revealing the employee's car park, miraculously untouched, protected by an impervious powerless metal gate. Sarah pressed the button on her keys and the bleep and blink of light from the car's central locking flashed a now alien sign of electronic life. She strapped the children to their seats and drove the car to the gate. A Range Rover was chosen. Sarah figured its battery would be the strongest. She was surprised by how easily the window broke. The children gasped when the window was smashed and held their breath as Sarah lugged the battery block to the gate then cheered with the snip, twist and rewiring that gave the first grind of the heavy gate wheels. Sarah's satisfaction sat short. As the world on the street revealed itself, she lost her smile and ran to the car.

They drove.

She told them not to look, but they did. They stayed with her in paralyzed silence, through all the disorder. She drove where she could, along roads, through parks and on footpaths. They saw death, drove around it, and drove away from it. How quickly the world had changed. Coco Pops one minute, car denting fury the next. They were not going home. There was nothing there for them. The only point of value, a hard drive of family photos, was now nothing but a useless chunk of plastic, swallowed along with the private history of millions of families around the world in a single digital gulp.

Sarah prayed the strength of her bond with Chris would give him a sense of where they were heading. She hoped desperately he would find them.

The family car made it out of the centre, bruised and battered, with three minds scarred forever. They took side roads, long cuts, avoided all traffic and contact. Cement finally gave way to grass and dirt, their paused breath, and blood began to flow once more. The children's voices returned with quiet and caution at first, ease seeping slowly behind it. When Jake asked "How much longer?" it felt as if the world was almost normal once more. Emily spotted the first cows, eating grass under the grey shadow of the eclipse as if nothing in their world had changed. The roads grew thinner, rougher and gravelled, just like they were meant to.

Sarah unlatched the gate, drove through, and latched it once more, as she had so many times before. The path was bumpy, overgrown, and uncontrolled. Leaves and branches sometimes swiped the car. Dry greenery broke suddenly open and the small cottage came into view.

"We're here!" cried Emily.

The front door opened and Sarah saw her mother's face, tired and worn. The exchanged embrace was silent and tear-filled. A large smiling dog loped forward to greet them and Emily and Jake raised their smiles in delight.

"Harry!" they screamed, chasing the four-legged lump of fur away from their mother's grasp.

Emily reached the tree first. She bent swiftly and scooped up the deep red fruit, swiping its surface with one hand before taking a giant crisp bite.

The small girl swallowed and turned to face Sarah, "Look Mummy, apples!"

Jasmine Yuen-Carrucan currently lives in Berlin with her family. She has written magazine articles about the films she worked on, or interviewed people she worked with. In 2008, she directed and wrote her first feature film, CACTUS, a road movie set in the Australian outback. She has written two more scripts since then. "Eclipsed" is her first venture into prose.

What You'll Find

Bri Hager

IF YOU WALKED UP TO the house at 21 Cross Crew Ave. in Fa Modega—twenty-three days from now, after we are long gone—you wouldn't know about the strange little playground that used to teeter and creak, filthy and proud, in the backyard. Or that me and my cousins used to pass the time by throwing an old hoola-hoop at the tall tree back there, making a game out of getting it stuck and working it out.

This was before the ozone layer collapsed. Before the world fell into a slightly deeper shade of shit. Before Scooby-Doo Band-Aids stopped helping the hurt. Before my parents' heads were pumped full of cancer clots from all the UV, and I used every last penny of their savings to purchase two one-way tickets on the rocket currently humming in the street—charring our already withered grass and throwing up white fingers of smoke that stretch and billow in the silver light of the moon.

After we are long gone, the stone fire pit that my father built that long summer ago might not last. Or the light sconces upstairs that my younger self always thought looked like mummy faces. The ghosts that'd sidled in my old bedroom; the stained glass suns my mom liked to make; the wonky wood benches my brother carved; the bits of things my parents always complained I left in my wake... The house may not growl so loudly at night, and you might not see us there at all.

Because the thing about running is that you always leave more than just the physical behind. You lose yourself. Bit by bit. Layer by layer. So you will never know the little girl who dropped to her knees when her first puppy hopped through the door; and again when he was carried out, old and sick. And, though I miss her, she's grown too heavy. Too petty. Too jaded and miserable and useless. So you will never know that she used to make her Nonna cook her animal-shaped pancakes, but then refused to eat them or even play with them. You will never know how many nights she and her dad spent outside, throwing the ball at midnight right after one of her games because she was unhappy with how she'd played. When the world was that easy to fix. When all it took was a little sweat and the drive to be better.

But you will feel us. You will feel us in the dents of the couch, where my mom liked to sleep with the faces of the TV glowing over her cheeks, hushing her to sleep. Or in the sad, little melody of the walls still humming pieces of the long-forgotten notes of my dad's vast singing. Or in the gentle quiet of a sister and her brother, no longer bickering.

If you walked up to the house at 21 Cross Crew Ave., even now, you would feel us like big laughter in an empty hallway. Not seen, not even heard, but tucked within every bent and soggy corner. Felt. In bright swaths of color. In strobe lights of raised voices. In the deep, sinking ink of unexplainable, dirty, messy love.

And you will find that this place was ours.

Bri Hager works in broadcasting for the New York Islanders, the New York Cosmos, and the Long Island Ducks. A recent college graduate, Bri holds a communications major. She secretly collects coffee mugs, but her true passion is writing. She loves the genres because these strange, little worlds are exciting and wonderful. Her story, "What You'll Find," won Metamorphose's Kick-Off Contest in the flash Sci-Fi category.

The Horrors of the Future

Leigh Patterson

MY NAME IS LEXI AND the year is 2464. Humanity is on the brink of extinction. I have found a small group of us left, resisting the aliens that have taken over our planet. We fight every day for our lives. The aliens are always one step ahead, waiting for us when we arrive at a new camp. There were at least 5,000 of us that began the resistance, but that number has now dwindled to ten. It began ten years ago when humanity thrived...

MY SISTER RAN AHEAD of me, but then suddenly turned and ran back. "Come on. Hurry up! I want to get home to see mum."

I sighed. "You've only been to school Emma. That's not too long. Mum will be just as she was when we left her this morning."

"Yeah but that's a whole six hours ago," she replied.

"Just go ahead and see her. I'll be fine by myself. I am nearly eighteen, you know." I shot back.

"Fine. I will, but if something happens to you don't blame me!" she snapped back.

I watched as she ran off ahead. And that was the last I saw of her. When I reached my house it was complete destruction. All that was left were several piles of bricks all placed in a hexagon three feet high. To my right was a body. I looked closer and saw it was my mother. I froze. My hand reached forward and touched her face. It was cold. She was dead. I was too shocked to cry. Suddenly, a gust of wind blew my hair in front of my face. I looked up and there it was: the first alien spaceship. I ran behind a wall opposite the street and watched as it landed on the piles of bricks. I gasped. It was huge and I was sure it was they who had killed my mother and sister.

"Keep your head down stupid girl," a voice hissed behind me. I whipped my head round to see Mr. Hendly, our elderly neighbor. "This has been planned for years, and one small child isn't going to stop them. Your mother and sister are gone. Dead. And you'll be going the same way if you're not careful." He hobbled back to the house with surprising speed for the age of him. I crouched and followed behind him, running to keep up. He then led me back into his house and I stood before a group of fifty people all from the surrounding area. Since then, I have been part of the human resistance and have been fighting the alien vermin.

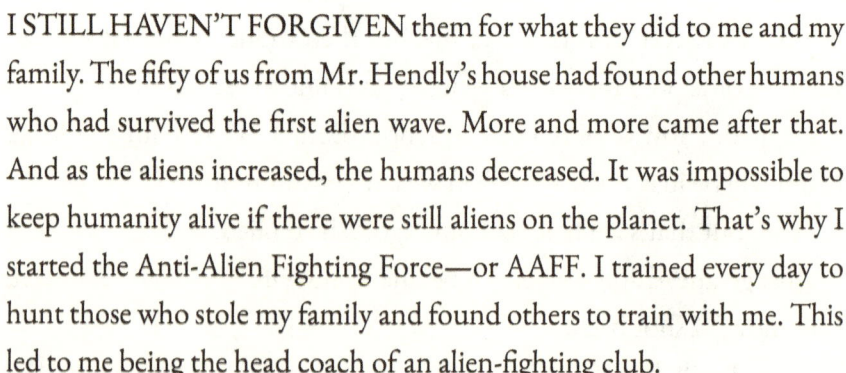

I STILL HAVEN'T FORGIVEN them for what they did to me and my family. The fifty of us from Mr. Hendly's house had found other humans who had survived the first alien wave. More and more came after that. And as the aliens increased, the humans decreased. It was impossible to keep humanity alive if there were still aliens on the planet. That's why I started the Anti-Alien Fighting Force—or AAFF. I trained every day to hunt those who stole my family and found others to train with me. This led to me being the head coach of an alien-fighting club.

WE TURNED THE CORNER and came face to face with five aliens. My hands tighten around the gun I had found, and I could feel the three others behind me tense up and prepare to fight. There was a moment when they registered that we were human and we readied ourselves for the attack. The aliens ran towards us, creating fireballs to throw. Was there anything that they couldn't do? I whipped the gun up and pulled the trigger. One fell with a thud and the others threw their fire. I dodged to the left and heard a scream behind me. Someone had been hit but there was no time to stop or we would all be goners. However, the scream reminded me of the danger, and I suddenly became blind with fear. I started to shoot anywhere in hope of hitting one of them. After five minutes, it went silent. I opened my eyes and looked around. The five aliens were dead and we had only lost one of us. This was the first time I had killed. But it was for the good of humanity.

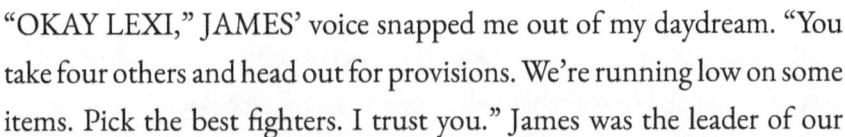

"OKAY LEXI," JAMES' voice snapped me out of my daydream. "You take four others and head out for provisions. We're running low on some items. Pick the best fighters. I trust you." James was the leader of our small group of ten.

I smiled softly back. "You got it, boss."

He leaned in and kissed me softly. "Hurry up. You know how nervous I get when you leave."

"Don't I always?" I reply laughing.

"Yep, and that's why I chose you each time." He responded, turned, and walked away with a look of amusement in his eyes. I knew how bad it affected him when I left the base camp. He would probably go and sulk until I was back. We had been close before the alien attack, but now the aliens had driven us into each other's arms. It was the best thing that had happened to me. I suppose that was one positive thing that came out of this whole experience.

"Right. Anna, Lucy, Sophie, and Ian. Follow me we're going out to get food." I shouted as I walked into the dining hall. The four stood up and walked silently to stand in front of me. I spun and started walking to the exit of the compound. Familiar with the procedure, the four that I had chosen hung back as I checked the area. I signaled that it was safe for them to follow and we ran to the storage unit where we kept supplies. Still, with no sound, we put purple-colored contact lenses in so we couldn't be recognized as humans. From this point on we wouldn't speak and risk being exposed as humans. The aliens had their own language, which we didn't know. It was frightening to think that I was trusted to lead a group of people—even after all this time—through a land full of danger that could lead to them death. The fear never leaves me.

One by one, we left the storage unit and found the track to the main road. From there we could easily find our way to a store and get our supplies.

It took us roughly half an hour to get to the road. We trudged along in silence until Lucy, who was about ten paces behind us, screamed. The rest of us turned to see what had happened. An alien had caught her.

This was it.

My fear had come true and someone would die because of me. I should have been the one behind and kept my eye on the others. The aliens looked strangely human, which made me uneasy. They must have stolen a body from one of us. How could they! The only way we could see that they weren't human was by their bright purple eyes. But once you were that close you were probably dead. Anna, Sophie, and Ian all ran toward her in a desperate attempt to save her. However, I knew that trying to help would wind up with me getting killed too. So I did what anyone in my shoes would have done.

Run.

As quickly as I had turned to look at Lucy, I turned and fled in the direction we were headed. They would all be discovered as humans and immediately killed. I couldn't face the thought of death. Not since the first day when I lost my family.

After running until I could run no more I stopped and looked back, nothing. No one had followed me. I allowed myself a short rest to get my breath back.

In the distance, I saw a floating sign. The vermin had brought their technology to our planet and it made me sick. Who were they to take over and suck our planet dry like parasites! I rose to my feet and limped toward the sign. My leg felt wet, and I looked down to see it pouring with blood. Judging by the size of it, I was going to need treatment soon or I wouldn't make it far before collapsing of blood loss.

Finally, I made it to the sign and found a small hotel below it. By this time I had formulated a plan: I would stumble in and then fall, hopefully causing the alien at the desk to call for help. I would then be transported to a hospital and helped. After that, I would sneak out and no questions would be asked. This involved no speaking and was perfect.

I burst through the door and immediately fell to the floor. There were screams and voices around me in a language that I did not understand. Suddenly, I was lifted up and placed on a soft bed. A cool hand was placed on my leg and the pain ended. Of course, they have healing powers. Why didn't I think of that? This made it much harder to escape. Slowly, I opened one of my eyes. They had all gone, and I was in what appeared to be a hotel room. Groggy, I sat up and climbed out of the bed.

My first thoughts were how to escape the room. I took in my surroundings and focused on the balcony. I hurried over and looked down. It was a ten-foot drop from here to the floor. I ran back to the bed, pulled the mattress off, and threw it over the balcony. Then the pillows. And the blankets. As I turned to survey the room one last time, I looked in the mirror. My eyes were still purple. Thank god they didn't notice that they were fake. If they did, then I don't think what I was about to do would work. I would be too closely watched. I walked back over to the edge of the balcony and looked down. The pile below was the softest landing that I was going to get.

Carefully, I climbed over the metal bars stopping me from falling. The metal was cool against my sweating palms. I grasped onto the lowest point I could, trying to reduce the distance. After a deep breath, I let go and started to fall. I clenched my jaw to try not to scream and alert the aliens inside of what I was doing. I landed and the wind was knocked out of me, but I had no time to recover. Immediately, I was on my feet and running from the hotel. I had to slow to a walk when I reached the main street and kept my eyes down.

I kept walking until the crowd around me started to thin. Until I was the only person on the road. This was when I brought my eyes up and looked at where I was. I must have been between two of their towns because there was nothing for miles around. I contemplated returning to the camp, but by this time they all would have been gone or dead. The latter was the most likely. My first love had been cruelly snatched from me just as my mother and Emma were. Their faces filled my head as I walked. I thought of all the times that we had spent together and a tear slipped down my cheek. That was it. That was the last thing those aliens steal get from me.

"Freeze and no one will get hurt," a voice yelled behind me. Finally, I was going to see my mother and sister again. Maybe dying wouldn't be too painful. I turned and sank to my knees, surrendering. I hoped that my immediate surrender would make my death less painful. There was no point fighting back. I was the last human. We had lost. Our planet was gone. A rough hand grabbed my chin and forced my head up. Slowly, I lifted my eyes. His eyes were clear blue; not purple. He was human. He saw my eyes and his hand tightened on the gun.

"Wait," I whispered. He stopped and confusion flashed over his face before it became hard again. I reached up and slowly took the contact lenses out. He looked shocked to find another human still alive. I smiled.

Leigh Patterson grew up in the north of England, feeding on books to keep her mind just as sharp as the rest of her. Her love for writing stems from her love for reading. Recently, she finished her A-levels and hopes to study the noble art of math at university. When not reading, she is either taking part in sports or catching up on her favorite shows. Leigh also has a passion for baking and enjoys making cakes.

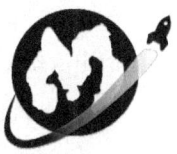

The Lunar Lifestyle

Rachel Anne Cantor

WE BOOKED THE CHEAPEST seats on the rocket, which meant that neither of us faced a window. If I craned my neck around, I could see the other couples sitting in the expensive seats, ogling at space and Earth through their window views. I didn't let it bother me. Once we got to the moon, everything would be free. I turned to Matt and pointed out a leftover drop of puke drying on his chin. He wiped it away with his sleeve. He didn't do so well with g-forces.

"Any regrets?" I asked him.

Matt shook his head. "We can always video chat my parents. Or your aunt. And we'll make new friends up here."

"I guess you're right."

"Besides, Clara, it's a fresh start. Think of it that way. A start for our family, you know?"

Matt yawned and thumbed through the Rocket Passenger Safety Handbook as we waited to disembark. It occurred to me that there was no point in reading the Rocket Passenger Safety Handbook at the conclusion of the trip. But he'd had a rough flight, so I didn't say anything.

Matt and I lived in Lake Placid, New York. Matt had taught sixth-grade math, and I'd taught seventh-grade geography. Eventually, they had to close the school because parents were getting concerned with the levels of radiation in the lake, so we signed up to go to the moon. Matt and I hadn't met at school, actually. He tells everyone that he fell in love with me at first sight. I'd stood out to him, apparently, in my bright green sundress on a warm winter's morning at the dentist's office. I've never had the heart or the courage to tell him that I'd only worn it because I'd been too lazy to do my laundry, and it was the only thing I'd had left. I certainly hadn't fallen for him as I waited to be de-plaqued. Matt had grown his bushy red hair out into a bushy red mustache back then. I considered it something of a public service when I made him shave.

Our rocket docked directly inside the lunar base. There were six or seven other bases scattered around the moon—China had one, as did Russia and a few other European countries—but Matt and I would be part of the first group to settle the new American base. The government had done surprisingly little advertising for the program. On the last day of school, our superintendent had simply handed us a flyer: "Married couples between the ages of twenty and thirty-five looking to start families." All expenses paid, forever. You just couldn't go back to Earth.

We stepped out of the rocket and into what I might have called an airport back on Earth. Robots that resembled forklifts unloaded everyone's scant luggage and whisked it away to our new homes. Our house turned out to be a clean, white, beach-style cottage. We were allowed a few hours to settle in before meeting the rest of the group for orientation. Most of the windows in our new home faced the street outside, but a small round one in our bedroom faced the dimpled landscape of the moon. I stared out of it as Matt unpacked the few clothes and mementos we'd been allowed to bring with us.

"Look, Matt," I said, pointing. "Earth." It hung there in the black sky just like the moon used to. I couldn't help but feel a sad little twinge. So far away. But I'd get used to our new life.

"What?" Matt said absently, busy hanging up pairs of pants in our new closet.

I sighed. Matt got this way sometimes—so focused on whatever task he'd set for himself that he went totally blind to everything else. I sometimes joked that I could burst into flame right in front of him and he might be too busy to notice.

"You can see Earth from here, that's all," I said. I gazed at it. Clouds had cleared over most of Africa and I could just make out the thin dusty patch of the Sahara. Behind me, Matt was making noise with the dresser drawers, slamming them open and shut as he loaded them with socks and underwear.

"Look at this," I said. I closed one eye and held my finger over the window. "I can cover all of Europe with my pinky finger." It made me feel very large and very tiny all at once. "Isn't that funny? Everything; everyone we've ever known is down there. It sort of takes my breath away, Matt." It really did. I had taught geography my whole career, but now I looked at Earth from beyond it. I felt a rush of adrenaline, and it made me a bit lightheaded. I'd never liked heights. And although I was on the ground floor of our new house in no danger of falling, I was suddenly, irrationally afraid.

"Yeah, Earth," Matt said. "Listen, Clara, we've only got an hour before we need to meet up with the rest of the group, and I want to get some of this done by then. Can you help unpack?" He pressed a few clothes hangers into my hands, impatient.

"Sorry," I said, shaking my head to clear it, "I'll unpack." I sat down at the edge of our vast new bed and unzipped my suitcase. The strange feeling passed, and I stole another glance out our window. I squinted at Africa. South of the Sahara, it was supposed to be grasslands. Wasn't it supposed to be greener?

Matt tapped my shoulder. "Where do you want to put our wedding photo?" He brandished the frame; our younger selves smiled in front of my face, blocking my view of the Earth.

"Maybe on that nice coffee table in the spare room? Matt, the Earth looks sort of gray. The land. I mean, I'm used to it looking so green. Like all the pictures in my classroom."

"I'm sure it just looks gray because you're looking at it through the habitation dome," said Matt. "And I'll put the picture in the living room. That's not a spare room, remember. It'll be a nursery one day!"

He left the room with the wedding picture and a few small items to place in the other rooms, which were pre-furnished. I'd gawked at the enormous white dining table, the polished granite kitchen countertops. Matt and I both said how much we loved having such nice, clean things, all for free, but part of me missed our shabby little home on Earth.

I heard Matt's footsteps on the stairs and turned away from the window, quickly hanging up a few blouses. I heard him whistling something without much of a melody. Homesickness was normal, but Matt wouldn't understand. When he came back into our room, he closed the curtains.

We finished unpacking and headed to the top of our street for orientation. I was feeling better—fresh air, I guess, even though I knew it was carefully regulated recycled oxygen. "Welcome, Moon Families!" a pink-and-blue banner proclaimed, strung up between two streetlights. The street itself was paved in precise square cobblestones, lined with parallel strips of artificial grass. The other houses were a variety of subdued beiges and blues, and they were all about the same size as ours. There were probably around thirty couples in our group; the rocket had seated one hundred. Everyone was very enthusiastic, and after a lot of introductions and chatting, my face hurt from all the smiling. A small robot appeared, wheeling a table with bowls of chips and pretzels. A chatty former nurse named Joanne convinced me to sign up for a weekly meeting group called Moon Mommy Mondays. It felt more like a neighborhood block party than an introduction to life off Earth.

AFTER AN HOUR OR SO of polite mingling, a petite blonde woman called the group to attention. "Welcome to American Lunar Base: Tranquility!" she chirped. "My name is Maria Norman, and I'm one of the researchers here. We'd like to welcome you to our Lifestyle Project. My husband Donnie and I will be participating right along with the rest of you Mommies-and-Daddies-To-Be!"Maria passed out a thick glossy white pamphlet with black cursive on the cover, "The Lunar Lifestyle Handbook."

Matt read the handbook fastidiously and encouraged me to do the same. It was full of cute aphorisms, followed by more in-depth guidelines for conduct in our Lifestyle Project. They ranged from "Left Your Job Behind on Earth? Find a Moon Hobby!" to "Sweet Ways to Avoid Spousal Conflict!" to "Thinking Maybe About Baby!"

American Lunar Base: Tranquility—ALBT, as everyone called it—had been built to look like a charming, small Earth town. All of the couples' quaint homes had artificial lawns, and the cobbled streets were lined with cheery streetlights, always switched on. An oxygenated habitation dome encapsulated the base. It had been specially designed to replicate Earth's gravity, and to keep us in a pleasant room temperature at all times. When I video chatted with my aunt back on Earth, I made it all sound very exciting and exotic—"Yes, we can see moon rocks out the window!"—when, in all honesty, it wasn't much different from living in a nice suburb set in perpetual nighttime. "What an adventure, dear!" my aunt said. "Your parents would have been so proud of you!"

Down the street from our house was the impressive faux-brick building which served as Health Headquarters. After a few months, with every passing pregnancy announcement from my new friends, I began to feel anxious.

"It's no rush, Clara," Matt reminded me. "'It's Not a Crime to Take Your Time!'" he said whenever I brought it up, citing the page in the handbook that discussed the so-called timeline of family planning. "They want us to behave as naturally as we would on Earth, to simulate what it would be like to live here, in case there has to be an Earth-wide evacuation."

"Matt, you don't think they would ever have to evacuate Earth, right?"

"Of course, not, Clara!" he said, laughing. "It's just precautionary. It can't hurt to have a settlement up here, that's all. On Earth, would we have jumped into intimacy and parenting, and all that, like rabbits?" He chuckled.

"Of course not, honey," I said whenever we had this conversation, and he would kiss the top of my head and tell me he loved me. I took to wearing the bright green dress from the first time he'd seen me, even though that had been almost six years ago now, and it didn't quite fit right on me anymore.

"You look lovely, sweetheart," Matt always said before he headed upstairs to his office to write math lesson plans for moon-born children, who would not be old enough to learn anything from us for another decade at least. There was no point in my planning any lessons. I'd taught geography—of Earth, and we'd left it. I did love Matt, too, of course.

We tried for a baby from time to time, but the lack of sun and proper Earth conditions could mess with the mind and body in many ways. That was all. This was what Maria and the other researchers were looking into. At the start of what would have been spring, I finally made an appointment with Maria at the clinic.

"I'm going to Joanne's baby shower," I called upstairs to Matt as I left the house. I felt a little bit bad about lying to him, but I couldn't exactly tell him the truth. I didn't want Matt to think I blamed him for our...lack of success. We'd had plenty of marital spats before, but none since we'd moved here, and I worried that such a delicate topic could ignite and explode in the tranquil space that had grown between us.

MARIA SAT ON THE DOCTOR'S stool across from my chair, her white lab coat hanging open, revealing a tank top stretched over the beginnings of a baby bump. For once, I was hyperconscious of having a flat stomach.

"You have a lovely home," Maria said, grinning at me, her huge teeth bleached bright white. "I can see it from that window," she said, pointing. "I love what you've done with the furniture layout in the bedroom."

Maria had done up her golden hair in flawless curls, and she wore pink eyeshadow. I ran a few fingers through my limp hair, and tried to pat the frizz down against my scalp. I felt more than a little nervous. I hadn't been wearing makeup lately. How old and mousy must I have looked, compared to her?

"So, are you ready to take the pregnancy test?" Maria asked, her grin widening even further.

"Oh—no, I'm definitely not—ready. I was actually wondering..." I stared at my hands to avoid Maria's sharp gaze and picked at my fingernails. "Well, Matt and I are having a bit of, you know, difficulty."

"Difficulty? Can you elaborate on that?"

"Yes, well, sure. Difficulty in terms of...conception."

Maria's face grew an expression of sympathy and she scooted towards me to take my hand, which immediately began to sweat.

"That is perfectly normal. Nothing to be ashamed of, especially for women towards the older end of the maternal spectrum. You're thirty-four, correct? Well, we can start you on—"

"No," I said, blushing, "I don't think there's anything I could take. The difficulty is in terms of... the bedroom. I think it might have something to do with Matt's... decreased blood flow, because of the lower gravity up here or something. Matt would have come to see you himself, but, um, he's very busy." My face burned. I looked at Maria's hand, curled around mine. Hers was tanned and manicured, with a tasteful diamond ring. My hand looked pale, gangly, dirty beneath my plain gold band, and I felt it grow clammier with each interminable second.

"Of course. Well, all of ALBT is gravity-controlled, as you know, but if I understand you correctly, what you have been struggling with is practically a nonissue. You should have seen me sooner!" Maria released my hand, finally, and got up to retrieve a pill bottle from the large medicine cabinet in the corner of her office. She pressed it into my clammy palms.

"Have Matt take one of these prior to initiating sexual intercourse, and be sure to call me if the erection lasts longer than two hours."

I spluttered a "thank you," as I tried not to stare at Maria's stomach, and excused myself from her office as fast as I could politely manage.

"You're so welcome, Clara." Her big smile stayed on her face as I closed the door.

That night, I crushed one of the blue tablets, stirred it into Matt's bedtime glass of milk, and waited. When we turned out the lights and got into bed, he clumsily rolled on top of me, and I didn't feel much except for a vague sense of emotional relief. Being with Matt had been more exciting when we first married. But, as the Lunar Lifestyle Handbook advised, "Enjoy the Hard Work of Marriage!" So I tried to.

Afterward, it occurred to me that what I'd done with the pills and the milk might have been a crime on Earth. I wasn't sure what the laws were here, come to think of it. It all made me a little uneasy. But nobody had to know. All our expenses were paid because we were part of a Family Lifestyle Project. It had to be done.

I passed a home pregnancy test shortly after the last blue tablet in the bottle had disappeared. "Share The Proud News That Baby Is Moon Bound!" advised the handbook, so I video chatted my aunt, and then put on my green dress to tell Matt. I wore it to my first official test and ultrasound at Health Headquarters, and Maria beamed at me.

I even tried to appreciate the violent vomiting episodes that seized me each dark morning. Morning sickness gave me something to do while Matt wrote his lesson plans and something to talk about with the other ALBT ladies when we all met for Moon Mommy Mondays at the Headquarters.

About eight months into my pregnancy, one afternoon—or maybe it was night, it was easy to lose track of the days under the constant black of the lunar sky—I was really craving fruit. I sat at the dining room table and stared at the fruit in the white glass bowl. It was always there, but neither Matt nor I had ever eaten any of it. Usually, we ate the prepackaged meals ALBT distributed every weekend; they were plenty filling. The fruit just sat there. It was all free, so we didn't feel the waste. Besides, we were rarely hungry anyway, not up here.

There were oranges, bananas, grapefruits. Bright tropical things I'd only ever seen in pictures. I mean, obviously the supermarket back in Lake Placid had sold fruit, but it never looked like this, all vibrant and ripe. Food hadn't looked so alive since I was a little girl. This fruit looked so good that it almost looked fake. Maybe it was?

I picked up a grapefruit and considered it in the palm of my hand. It almost glowed neon orange, so bright against the white of our walls and the dull dark of the galactic sky. It was real. I was going to peel it. It felt sort of sneaky. It felt a little like stealing. Why was that? Everything belonged to me—to us. ALBT itself was government property, sure, but the things they had given us were ours. Our house, our clothes, our food—this fruit. Still, I shifted in the plush dining room chair and glanced over my shoulder. Nothing there but the blank wall. I still wasn't used to luxury like this. That was all. On Earth, Matt and I hadn't had a dining room table, let alone fruit to put on it, and that was why it felt like all these new things were too good to truly be mine.

I turned back to the table. It was silly and paranoid to feel that I was being watched. It was probably just the effect of having another person growing inside my body—or maybe it was just the population of Earth, staring up at the moon.

"It's my f—" I was about to curse, but remembered the handbook's warning: "Don't Curse In Front Of Your Fetus! Unborn Ears Can Still Hear!"

"It's my fruit," I amended. "I am going to eat my darn fruit."

I jabbed my thumb into the taut skin of the grapefruit, and it splattered my fingers with a spray of red juice. For half a second it looked like there was blood on my hands. I pulled the grapefruit open. It was rotten; a black mold was rooted at the center of the fruit and growing outwards. It smelled awful. I dropped it onto the flat white of the dining table and it oozed more red.

When I peeled them, all the ripe, golden bananas were black with malignant bruises on the inside. I grabbed the roundest, brightest orange, ripped it in two; it was even worse. Its mold was a gray-green slime.

All of it was rotten and dead. My hands reeked of it, stained deep red and black and green with ruined fruit and mold; without thinking I wiped them on my t-shirt, against my belly. Then the fetus kicked.

But it couldn't be a fetus now; it was a baby, a real live thing. It kicked me again from the inside and pain shot up my spine and through my whole body.

"Matt," I said. The baby kicked harder when I said his name. "Matt." He still did not hear. I heard blood rush in my ears as I shoved the chair out from behind me and staggered to my feet. The baby didn't like me moving. It felt like it had claws. I sank to the white tile, or maybe I fell, I'm not sure. In the haze above my eyes, I saw Matt's reddish form standing over me. The baby was coming. It had been everything I wanted—but now I wanted it all to stop.

"Clara! What on Earth did you do to our fruit?!" He looked at me for a moment, puzzled, and then he ran for the kitchen phone.

The next thing I remembered was Maria's voice. "Clara? Clara, sweetie, there was a little issue and we had to do a C-section, okay? But the baby is doing great—that's right, you're a Moon Mommy! Congratulations!"

Matt came into focus, his eyes full of tears, his crimson hair standing up at funny angles as if he'd been tugging at it. He held a small bundle in a blue blanket.

"Clara, darling," Matt said, breathless, leaning towards me with the blue bundle. His tall form swayed slightly. Everything was muffled and blurry, as if I'd slipped underwater. I couldn't see the baby's face. "Clara... Matt Jr.?"

"Yes," I managed, my voice sounding rather far away. "That's fine."

What had gone wrong was never fully explained to me. Maria kept repeating that it had been a blood flow issue, just a pregnancy side effect, maybe due to my age, nothing to worry about, nothing I could have done differently. Still, I was kept on strict bed rest for a while. Matt was very helpful with me and Matt Jr. He wouldn't let me so much as change a diaper. He even whisked the baby out of the room if he started to cry. One of the other new mothers nursed Matt Jr., so that I wouldn't have to. Matt reminded me how lucky we were that these complications had happened on the moon, where everything was free and lots of people could help. Still, when I wiped the wasted milk off my nightgown, I sometimes found it hard not to cry.

At Maria's suggestion, a string of my new friends from Moon Mommy Mondays came to relieve Matt for a few hours every day, to sit with me and babysit. They were lovely, of course, and I thanked them profusely for the company and help. But sometimes it was hard to fill such a long day with constant conversation. Matt reassured me that it was just the recovery, and that I would be more cheerful soon. I would turn over to one side in the bed that Matt no longer slept in—I appreciated that he slept on the couch for my health—feign sleep, and stare at the sliver of moonscape and space I could see out of the bedroom window.

One day, after Joanne had put Matt Jr. down for his nap, she got a call from her husband: one of her twins had pushed the other out of the playhouse and given him a nosebleed.

Joanne hung up and turned to me. "Don't you lift a finger, honey!" she said. "There's no need to go to the baby if he cries while I'm out. Like Maria says, it's best that Matt and the Mommies tend to him for now. You'll get better sooner without that stress. Rest up. I'll see you in a few minutes, Clara!"

I wanted to shout at her that lately, I had been feeling more stressed than rested, and that I was perfectly capable of holding my own child. But if I was honest, I'd barely touched Matt Jr., and I was afraid those maternal instincts the other women had always mentioned at Moon Mommy Mondays wouldn't work. Like muscles that atrophy without use. My baby seemed distant and alien, barely mine. Most of the time I tried not to let myself think it, but I couldn't help it. I was afraid of him.

I heard our front door close and realized it had been weeks since I'd been alone. Slowly, I sat up. I felt fine. I had to get out of bed, out of this room, out of this house, or else I might scream. I slipped out from under the covers, testing myself, daring the floor to creak and give me away. But I moved silently out of the room. I tiptoed past Matt's office, down the stairs, and out our front door. I wasn't quite sure where I was going, but I didn't want to risk anyone catching sight of me, so I headed toward to the back of the house, my nightgown billowing around my thighs in the artificial breeze. I tried to run, but the thin-lipped grimace of a scar threatened to tear open my abdomen and bleed, so I walked. My slow steps gave me the sensation I often felt in nightmares: the need to run, except you can't—your body seems too heavy and your legs won't move, and the terror lurking in the distance is just about to arrive.

I walked past our patio, down our fake-grass lawn, and down the decline beyond it, until I was close enough to touch the surface of ALBT's habitation dome. The ground was cold and strange on my bare feet. Shivers coursed through my body as I reached towards the edge of the dome, and I hoped the glass wasn't electrified. I looked across the gray moon at the small Earth turning in the distant void. Earth looked even grayer, sicker than the last time I'd looked at it when we'd first landed on the moon. I beat against the glass with both fists, realizing that I was screaming; it wasn't breaking. I couldn't get out.

I turned around and looked back through the windows of our house. I saw Matt rocking Matt Jr. at the edge of his crib. My baby turned his head and looked at me, his puff of fiery hair a miniature model of Matt's. I knew I should smile at him, but his dark eyes stared at me as if he knew I was a stranger. Something caught in the back of my throat.

"Your baby is just the cutest little thing!" Maria said, walking over to stand next to me. It dawned on me that she had seen everything, this whole time—she could look inside my house from her office. And it was then that I knew it was not my house. Not my town. ALBT had never been a town. We were being watched, and we'd been watched this whole time. It was an experiment, and I was a rat in the cage.

Slowly, I lowered my hands from the impenetrable glass and clasped them over my nightgown, over the cut in my abdomen. My hands were shaking, and I knew that I would never be without the hushed fear that had grown in me in these past few months, like a parasite.

"I just want to squeeze that darling little boy," Maria cooed at me, grinning with those big white teeth. "I hope he and Donnie Jr. can be friends when they grow up." She stroked her belly, round with another pregnancy. "And this one, too. I want to have as many as I can, don't you?"

I took one final look at the dying Earth, then turned to face her. I tried to clear my throat, but the fear still sat there; heavy, choking me slowly.

"Of course I do," I lied.

Rachel Anne Cantor is a nineteen-year-old sophomore at Emerson College in Boston, MA, where she is pursuing a BFA in Writing, Literature, and Publishing, with a minor in History. When she's not at school, Rachel lives in New Jersey and works in New York City. She currently interns for Liza Dawson Associates Literary Agency, as well as Bearport Publishing. Rachel began writing fiction when she was five years old. Since then, she's loved to read and write in any genre.

Sher's Wood

Jack Dowd

"FORTY-SEVEN THOUSAND POUNDS OF food supplies," Gisborne said motioning to the hologram of the Docking Bay. He watched the Sheriff study the images of the landing cargo vessels, their contents displayed on a separate projection.

The Sheriff said nothing.

"We've already bombed half the planet. Our estimate is that it'll take us another hour to finish the run." Gisborne pressed a button on his remote and the projection was replaced by a squad of pilots performing start-up processors inside their ships. Gisborne watched as they tested their comms link and adjusted the controls in the cockpit.

The Sheriff remained silent.

Masking his frustration, Gisborne explained the details of the raid—which had been plotted over several months—and awaited a reaction. When he had finished, the Sheriff lazily deactivated the holodisk and slumped back in his chair.

"Call back the pilots and send me the report by tomorrow. I think we're done here." The Sheriff returned his attention to the monitor on his desk.

"Y-yes sir." Gisborne scooped up his helmet, snapped to attention, and saluted.

This office should be mine.

How could the King have placed this bloody psychopath in charge? Gisborne had searched the ship's database shortly after the Sheriff's promotion. War hero, veteran. These were clearly lies written by the Sheriff and uploaded as fact.

"Why are you still here?"

"Sorry sir." Gisborne's jaw clenched, and he withdrew from the office.

He glanced across the control bridge manned by fifty officers, each bathed in the artificial light of their work stations encompassing the main control hub. Here, the senior officers gathered around the holoplatform displaying the projection of Sher's Wood and were overseeing the attack. Gisborne relayed the Sheriff's order to a senior officer and watched as the man barked out commands to his subordinates. Gisborne spotted several cadets gathered by the viewing port to watch the destruction firsthand. He joined them.

A smokescreen covered the atmosphere of the planet, shielding it from the sun's rays. Red pulses of light beneath the smoke told Gisborne that the bombing run was still in progress. The forest that occupied the surface of the planet was an inferno, and countless natives would perish in those flames.

We're nowhere near finished with that rock.

So what if the Sheriff wanted the people alive to pay taxes? He could find the money elsewhere. The rebels on Sher's Wood would fight back. True, they possessed little technology, Gisborne doubted a single ship would survive the fire but they could always send a transmission for help. Someone would answer.

We should kill them all before they attempt another uprising.

Strapping on his helmet, Gisborne marched toward the lift doors. The pilots would need to be debriefed and dismissed upon their return. He activated the radio comm concealed within his helmet and switched to a private channel.

"Marian, you there?"

After several heartbeats, she answered, and Gisborne allowed himself a smile.

"Yes, what happened? What did the sheriff say?" He could hear the panic in her voice and could imagine her pouted lips.

"Not a lot. We only burned half the planet but we're calling the pilots back now." He hesitated. "I can pop by later on if you like?"

Marian's answer was lost as The Nottingham lurched.

Gisborne collapsed against the lift doors. Warning alarms blared across the bridge, followed by the clatter of objects falling from workstations. The senior officers bellowed at the juniors who had yet to return to their feet, too dazed to understand what had happened.

Gisborne scrambled upright.

"Guy?" Was that panic in her voice? "Guy, can you hear me?"

"I'm fine," Gisborne snapped, "Stay in your quarters until I call you, okay?"

"Yeah, what's going on?"

He wanted nothing more than to escape to Marian's quarters, hold her tight, feel the warmth of her body, and tell her everything would be alright but the Sheriff tumbled out of his office.

"What the bloody hell was that?" he roared, as if it were Gisborne's fault.

"Someone's rammed us, Commander," a female officer said from her station.

"Who?" The sheriff yelled.

"It's an unidentified craft, Commander. Portside."

"Show it on the holoplatform," Gisborne ordered.

"Yes General."

There was a click from the comms as Marian terminated the call, and Gisborne felt a swell of disappointment.

Two projections blinked into existence above the control hub. The first image was of The Nottingham. Her control spires and metallic hull were rendered in perfect detail. The second ship was dwarfed beside her. A cargo hopper, less than a tenth of the size of The Nottingham. Several lights, which Gisborne understood to be missiles, leaped from the second ship and exploded midway down The Nottingham.

"Shoot it down," the Sheriff screamed as the bridge jerked.

"We can't, sir," the officer said. "It's too small a craft for our guns to lock on to."

The ship zoomed away. Perhaps to line up another shot.

Gisborne noted the fear in the Sheriff's voice. "Load up the schematics of the ship. I want to see where they're hitting us," he ordered, "and someone call the fighters on Sher's Wood. Tell them to engage."

The images of the two ships were replaced by the blueprints of The Nottingham. A small section of the hull, midway down the ship, flashed red. Gisborne uttered a silent prayer of thanks that Marian wasn't in that sector. He pinched the air near the damaged section. The image zoomed in.

"We can't contact the fleet sir," an officer called. "Our communications to the planet are jammed."

The Nottingham trembled once more.

Gisborne fell against the control hub, his elbow brushing the standby button. The projection powered down. The Sheriff attempted to cling to the controls but only succeeded in knocking over the female officer next to him. She fell across his lap. Gisborne rebooted the projection as the ship settled.

The Sheriff shoved the officer off him and looked at the projection.

"Isn't that the Cargo Bay?" he asked.

Gisborne nodded. Twenty cargo ships stood on the deck, each anchored to the ground by individual gravity wells. Their crews had long since fled.

Why the hell do they keep hitting us there?

"Tell the mechanics to converge in the bay to repair the damage," Gisborne said to a scarlet-faced officer. "I'll meet them there."

He sprinted into the lift and was able to watch the Sheriff overbalance again before the doors closed.

TWO CADETS FRANTICALLY worked the controls as Gisborne entered. He glanced at the door out of the control room, which led down to the bay via a staircase. Locked. Aside from two chairs, the viewing ports looking over the bay, and the two cadets, the rest of the control room was filled with consoles flashing warnings and alarms.

How have the pirates managed to freeze the controls? They can't have got past our firewalls.

"General, what do we do?" one of the cadets squealed.

"Are the mechanics here yet?"

"No, why?"

Gisborne ignored the man and tried to flick a switch on the controls. He scowled at the unresponsive machinery.

The second cadet pointed at the wall above the hanger doors. A section of the hull had buckled inwards.

That's where the pirates are striking. They're going to raid us.

Gisborne checked the ship's vitals displayed in his helmet. The pressure stabilized. Clearly, the pirates did not seek to destroy the ship. The thought brought small comfort.

"Go and get help," Gisborne ordered, turning to the cadets. "Anyone, anyone with a weapon. We're going to be raided, understand?" The cadets nodded and fled down the corridor. They never expected to see combat. They weren't prepared to mount a defense. Gisborne pitied them. The door closed behind the pair with a thud, followed by a clang. Locked.

Gisborne waved at the door sensor and issued a command code into his comms. No response. Silently cursing, he flicked on an open channel.

"Can anyone hear me? I'm locked in the Cargo Bay Control Room. I say again I'm locked inside the Cargo Bay. We're going to be raided." His voice joined the other hundreds that were crying out for help.

A single ship can't do this much damage. A single ship shouldn't have bypassed our shields. He flicked to a private channel.

"Sheriff?"

"Gisborne. Where are you?"

"'The Cargo Bay. They're about to raid us, sir. I need armed personal here. And the mechanics."

"The comms are shutting down," the Sheriff responded. "The doors have locked themselves."

What, all of them, Gisborne wanted to say.

He studied the ships below, still loaded with food from Sher's Wood. Hardly a prize.

"Unlock the doors," he snapped into his comm.

"I can't!"

Gods, please keep Marian safe. If all the doors were locked, she should remain safe in her cabin.

The damaged section of the hull blasted into the Bay. Gisborne flinched despite the knowledge that the Control Room's doors were airtight and a supply of oxygen was being pumped into the room by the Life Support Systems. Debris flew above the ships before being sucked into space, along with every object not bolted down to the deck. The cargo ships' landing arms scratched the durosteel floor as their gravity wells faltered. Then the vacuum ceased and the few pieces of shrapnel that hadn't been blasted into space clattered across the deck.

An amber shield plugged the breach. Gisborne stared at it.

"Gisborne, what's going on?"

The shield pulsed like a heartbeat. Gisborne realised what it was. A gravity corridor. It stretched from the hanger bay toward the pirate's ship. He watched through the viewing port as something whizzed down the corridor, shot across the bay, and connected with the adjacent wall. Gisborne's mind had just time to accept it was a cable as the first pirate zip-wired into view.

"Gisborne, can you hear me?"

The pirate scanned the deck as the corridor rippled behind him, he used a bow to ride down the cable and across the bay. The insignia on the arm of his emerald armourweave identified him as a solider, but of what class and rank Gisborne couldn't determine. Aside from the quiver-like tube strapped to his back, Gisborne couldn't see any other weapons. The pirate dropped from the cable, his boots hitting the steel deck with two loud clacks.

"Gisborne!" The Sheriff growled through the comms, but Gisborne failed to answer.

The invader scanned the deck for any resistance. Finding none, he spoke into a communicator hidden beneath his hood.

Five more men zip-wired into the bay. Each was dressed identical to their leader, with the exception that they all carried crossbows on their belts.

There's only six of them...

The bowman held his hand to his ear and then pointed to the Control Room. His men charged the stairs, drawing weapons.

"They're coming for me."

"Well, kill them," the Sheriff snapped.

"It's five on one!"

"You have a gun, don't—" The channel died.

Gisborne fumbled with the grip on his blaster, then aimed his weapon at the door.

Crack!

He flinched. The viewing port fractured. Cracks ran from the centre of the hyperglass to the edge, threatening to shatter. Something long and thin was sticking out of the other side.

Is that... an arrow?

The shaft of the arrow slid back to reveal a grill. A high-pitched whine screeched across the Bay.

The shrill sound drilled into his skull. He screamed to drown out the noise, dropping his blaster to clamp his ears, but only succeeded in making his throat raw. After several seconds, the torture ended. The viewing port shattered. The arrow fell to the deck below as shards of glass rained down onto the floor of the Control Room.

Gods...

Gisborne crushed broken glass underneath his boots as he rose.

Thump.

A second arrow flew through the broken viewing port and struck the Control Room wall. Gas erupted from the nock of the arrow. Gisborne leaned on the controls to push himself to his feet. He covered his mouth with his sleeve, but could already feel the effects of the gas. The little strength that remained began to wane. His vision faded.

VOICES.

The words were incoherent, elapsing into each other.

Gisborne blinked. His vison returned. The bowman was smiling down at him.

"Awake, are we?"

The first thing Gisborne noticed was the man's skin. Flawless. Gisborne couldn't locate a single spot or pimple. He felt more aware of his own body covered in oil, grease, and sweat. The man's hazel eyes matched his trimmed beard. His teeth were a near-perfect white and his hair was thick with gel. Gisborne thought he wouldn't look amiss in one of those romantic films Marian was fond of watching.

The others laughed, and Gisborne realised he was surrounded. They had tied him to a chair in the corner of the Control Room. The cable dug into his wrists and ankles. He tried to speak but his mouth wouldn't form the words he wanted.

The leader patted Gisborne on the shoulder, sending a shockwave of pain through his body. Laughing, the Bowman pressed a button on the control panel. The loading ramps on the cargo ships descended to the deck. "Why don't you watch us take back that food until you feel better?" The man smirked.

Laughter echoed around Gisborne. The pounding in his head increased.

"Keep an eye on him, John," the bowman ordered. The largest of the raiders nodded and wheeled Gisborne toward the remains of the viewing port as the rest of the pirates left.

How did they break through the door?

Peering past the giant man that guarded him, Gisborne spotted another arrow above a space of partially melted metal in the door frame.

That looks like acid. Acid arrows? He had never seen such weapons before.

"Do you see that?" John asked, pointing down to the bay. Gisborne didn't attempt an answer.

"I said, do you see that?" The chair slammed against the controls. Spots clouded Gisborne's vision. "Do you see all that food you stole from Sher's Wood?"

Gisborne watched as one of the pirates fired a gravity gun into the hold of a ship. A whisper of light stretched from the nozzle of the gun and wrapped itself around the crates of food. The pirate worked the controls on the gun, maneuvering the food toward the gravity corridor. As the food touched the amber light, it drifted along the corridor toward the pirate's ship.

"People could have died today," John continued. "You and your men could have killed thousands."

Gisborne managed a grunt. Could have died? They did. They died. We burned their forest.

"If they hadn't taken shelter underground, they would all be dead. Men, women, and children. How do you feel about that?"

Underground? How could they have had time to build shelters? They didn't know about the bombing run, they couldn't have done. Unless... We must have a leak.

Gisborne made a mental list of the officers who had the details of the operation but failed to believe any of them were turncoats. The planning of the pirate's attack. The effectiveness. Somebody wanted to make a statement against the Sheriff.

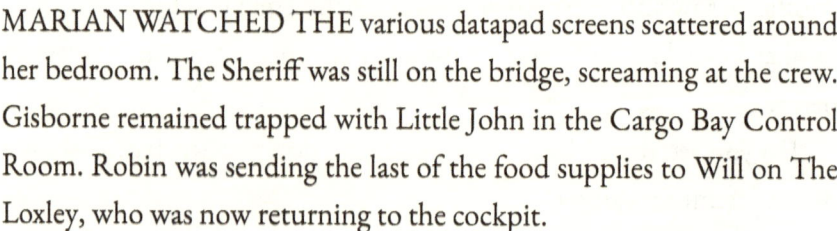

MARIAN WATCHED THE various datapad screens scattered around her bedroom. The Sheriff was still on the bridge, screaming at the crew. Gisborne remained trapped with Little John in the Cargo Bay Control Room. Robin was sending the last of the food supplies to Will on The Loxley, who was now returning to the cockpit.

"Marian, we're all clear," Will said, "Give Robin the heads up."

"Right. I'll tell him now."

She glanced at a scanner displayed on one of the screens. Apart from The Loxley and The Nottingham, there wasn't another ship in view. The bombers were still in Sher's Wood's atmosphere. Communications between them and The Nottingham were disabled by Marian's hand, along with the external shields.

"Robin, Will says it's all loaded up. Time to go."

Please don't gloat. Please just once. Just once in your life do as you're told.

"Okay, everyone back to the ship," Robin said.

The screen of the Cargo Bay showed Allen, Much, Tuck, and Djaq pulling the zip-wire out of the wall. Robin, however, was racing up the stairs to the Control Room.

Gisborne. Poor thing. He tried so hard.

"Let's go," she heard Robin order John. It hadn't escaped her notice that Gisborne had been eyeing his blaster, no doubt plotting a way to reach it.

"Do you know who I am?" Robin said, his voice clear over her comms.

Gisborne shook his head, and Marian thought she could see the fear in his eyes.

"My name is Robin Hood, and everyone on Sher's Wood or any planet in this quadrant is under my protection. You got that? Sher's Wood is defended."

Gisborne nodded.

Marian watched Robin load his bow and aim the arrow at Gisborne's head. The fear was no longer masked. Gisborne writhed in his seat.

Twang!

Robin stood over his captive grinning, the arrow embedded in the chair. Marian couldn't contain a giggle. It was followed by a pang of guilt that was swiftly obliterated when she remembered what Gisborne had said.

We only burned half the planet...

"Sleep tight." Robin smirked.

Marian watched as the knockout gas hissed around Gisborne before switching her attention to the screen of the Cargo Bay. Little John had taken his place among the outlaws clutching the fallen cable.

"Tell Will we're ready," Robin ordered as he took a hold of the cable.

You didn't have to do that to him, Marian thought. Robin treated everything as a game.

"Will, they're ready to go."

The cable tightened and dragged the men along the deck. Marian watched as they scaled the Cargo Bay wall and leaped into the gravity corridor before remerging on The Loxley's Holding Bay.

Will pulled a lever and the gravity corridor vanished. The Nottingham's Life Supports System detected the breach in the hull instantly. A spare millenniumsteel plate shunted into the gap to maintain pressure. On Marian's screens, The Nottingham looked like a ghost ship. Abandoned. Dark. Left to float in space.

"Do you want me to pop by when you're rescued?" Robin asked.

Marian smiled. "That'll be perfect." She heard him laugh as The Loxley's engines flashed and sent the ship into hyperspace.

Marian turned the power back on with a jab of a button. The doors unsealed. The lighting throughout the ship reactivated, and with a few more presses all radio frequencies were re-established. The shields came back online. The hangers reopened and the engines restored themselves to full working order. Radio channels blared with life. Marian paused before adding her own voice to the mix.

"Has anyone seen my husband?"

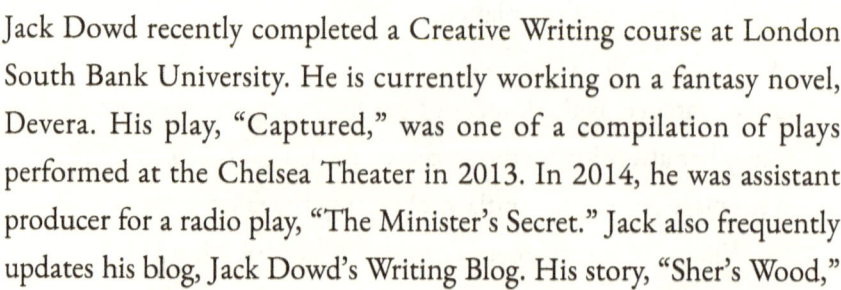

Jack Dowd recently completed a Creative Writing course at London South Bank University. He is currently working on a fantasy novel, Devera. His play, "Captured," was one of a compilation of plays performed at the Chelsea Theater in 2013. In 2014, he was assistant producer for a radio play, "The Minister's Secret." Jack also frequently updates his blog, Jack Dowd's Writing Blog. His story, "Sher's Wood,"

won first place in Metamorphose's Kick-Off Contest in the Short Sci-Fi category, and was selected as a featured cover story.

Pebble Baby

Brandon Bigard

WAKING UP, SHE WALKED down to the water. There was a pebble-shaped ball and it had a heartbeat. Oddly, she felt attached, but she didn't want to take it home. She walked further into the water and placed it between two rocks, happy that it was safe for her to get later.

Week 1.

She came back, her urge to go to the water odd since she was not thirsty. She was, however, shocked to find that her little "thing" had changed. It was the color of a peach, and it was making more of a slight heartbeat sound. She felt that she wanted to do something with the small ball, but she still felt she wasn't ready to take it home. So she walked out even further and buried it under the sand. Once again feeling content, she walked away knowing that she was the only one that would know where it was.

Week 5.

She came back in tears, her feelings made her murky in thought as she stumbled back to the water. Her day was horrible, and no one seemed to care that she existed. She felt alone until she remembered the little ball that she buried. She raced to the little ball in horror, hoping that the clay-like sand under the water did not crush the little ball due to her burying it. She rushed into the water, teary-eyed with apologies on her tongue. There was a moment of surprise when she pulled up a pulsating, soccer ball-sized thing that pulsated in her hand-colored a deep purple.

She cried and tried to wash the ingrained pieces of sand within it until they were all clear. She cried and held it, kissing it until night came. Then she walked down even further into the water, the soft waves lapping at her neck as she used her feet to create a cradle-like ditch in the sand, placing the ball down carefully.

Walking back, she realized that she would not talk to anyone about the ball, as she was the only one she wanted to know about it and want it.

Week 8.

She had come regularly, noting that the color changed from purple to green to yellow to teal. Each time she came she was surprised at the color. But now she was getting used to the color change, and she was happy to see the changing colors again. She also realized that it was getting clearer with every color change, showing a peek at the life form that she wanted to see. Those whom she was around were confused by her sudden obsession to the water, but she would not let them bug her or upset her anymore. She just wanted to see how this would end. Quietly.

Pulling out the exercise ball-sized globe was something she loved to do, rolling it to the shore as she was shown its new color slowly. She sat down by the shore to hug and kiss the globe using her whole body to hold it to her, the pulsating now synced to her own heartbeat.

She pressed her face to the globe, listening to what was inside pushing and moving against her questioning hands. She pressed her face to the globe and tried to peek at what was moving inside. A small smile graced her lips as she moved the ball back into place.

Week 9.

No one wanted her to come today as the storm brought the water closer to the shore, but she had to go to it. The globe was calling to her and she felt the pain of not answering it. She walked to the water calmly as the wind whipped around her and the water threw its icy fingers around her.

She didn't care though. She walked calmly down into the water, pushing the globe further in as the water went over her head.

A few hours later, people came out to see what had happened to her as they followed what remained of her footsteps.

They were ready to mourn her when she appeared coughing and gasping as she held something close to her. They dragged her out the rest of the way, turning her around to see what she had in her arms.

They were surprised to see a small little form wiggling in her arms and her smiling down at it. The small sounds amazed them as she stood up from the sand and the waves crashed against her thighs. With a smile, she began walking home, finally carrying with her what she had found in the water.

As she passed, pebble-sized balls fell from her shirt as she walked.

Brandon Bigard lives in New Orleans, Louisiana. Stories hold a dear place in Brandon's heart, and have for as long as she recalls being told stories. Her passion for fantasy and sci-fi stems from the belief that the past, the future, the real, and the imagined collide when you write in the genres. You feel what your character is feeling and believe that anything is possible. It's uplifting and scary; the perfect combo for a good life.

From Misfortune, A Voyage

Juan Paulo Rafols

IT WAS MISFORTUNE THAT gave birth to the idea—that idle notion that would carry me away from family, tribe, and the nostalgic shores of Ato.

In the wake of the tempest season, that period of lustful liaison between Sky and Sea, the men of Ato would skim their canoes over the reef. It was then that the deep fish mated on the shoals, fat and succulent beneath their resplendent orange-white scales. Nets would tear on jagged coral; instead, we pierced the water with spear and trident, thrusting with hearty cries of 'Ora!'

At times, fitful Sky would thunder in the aftermath of his lovemaking. During those temperamental evenings, we would race the tide to the shore and huddle beneath broad leaves until the clouds released their embrace. On one such afternoon, Etiki the Younger misjudged the current and beached his canoe on a cruel curve of jeweled coral.

The men on the shore, myself included, waded out to help. We trod the barely-visible path of rough coral, every two steps pausing to brace ourselves against the rush and ebb of tide. We lined ourselves, a half dozen on either side, and hugged the canoe with our salt-slippery arms. We heaved and we swore and we shouted, but Sea would not relinquish her prize. By the time clouds parted to rosy dusk, we were sprawled, defeated, on the beach, nursing the cut soles of our feet.

Etiki the Younger was despondent. He stood alone, thigh-deep in water, watching the canoe carved by his family slowly subsumed in the tide.

Moved, perhaps, by his solitary silence—or, more likely, annoyed by our defeat at the hands of willful Sea—I stood and beat the wet sand off my thighs. "Brother," I said, addressing my older cousin Tiantu, "help me bring your canoe next to mine."

Tiantu accompanied me to where our own boats were beached on the shore. Initial hesitation gave way to understanding as he watched my labor. He knelt by me and we lashed our two canoes together by the midsection. His mast we removed; mine we folded. The other men gathered and helped us push. Our twin canoes made one, launched against the tide, and cut into it. Tiantu and I lay on our stomachs on the two prows, paddling.

Our make-shift craft, lashed together as it was by rope and driftwood, skimmed over shoals. Nervously, I perceived the impossible closeness of the reef beneath, my paddle sometimes striking coral and shoving off. Nonetheless, our twin hulls slid over the tide like a pond-dwelling waterwalker, and we soon found ourselves close to Etiki's stranded boat. Tiantu disembarked and lashed it to the aft of our craft.

I unfolded the creaking mast and the wind caught us. We were unbalanced, of course, but our tilt carried us to the shore. I listened to the strain of rope and hull, tense until Etiki's canoe broke free with a shriek of scraping wood. My cousin echoed my whoops and hollered success all the way to shore, where we tumbled off into sand and a hubbub of excited voices.

Tearful Etiki embraced me, unmanly but sincere in his gratitude. The events of that evening gave the men of Ato an excuse to forgo fishing and instead celebrate around a beach bonfire, drinking the fermented sap of coconut flower until the women finally dragged or shamed them home.

"WE CAN BUILD SHIPS like that. Twin hulls," I told Iriti the Older, as the shipbuilder circled our lashed-together canoes the next morning, surveying our ad-hoc craft. Iriti the Older was a kahuna in his own right, a master known as far windward as the Twelve Isles.

The broad-shouldered man, proudly bearing the tattoos of his station from shoulder to wrist, patted the prow of my canoe. His eyes danced over the hull in thought.

"A frame in the center for the sail," I continued. "Tallwood, or..."

"Dryshined bamboo," he finished. I knew that the experienced shipbuilder had considered all this, and more. My words were meant to prod, not to inform. Iriti added, "The hulls can be thinner, sharper. Closed. If the morning wind abandons you, you'll be in trouble..."

"But I won't heel as much, tacking." I countered. "And the drought is shallow."

"Very shallow," Iriti agreed, squatting to inspect the scrapes on the hull.

"Shallow enough to cross the Shark's Teeth," I suggested.

That drew Iriti's attention, as well it should. A half-circle of reef ringed Ato in the direction of Sun's climb, stretching for countless leagues in both directions. One can venture windward to the Singing Cliffs and the dock-towns of the Mur. Or one can follow the current to the Always-Green, where the painted kings ruled from whalebone thrones. But no one can follow Sun's rise from Ato—the Shark's Teeth were too shallow, the currents too capricious. None have returned from such a venture; all sensible seafarers regarded Ato as the edge of the world.

Predictably, Iriti the Older stood and gave me a look that told me I was crazy.

"You're crazy," he said, making sure the message got across.

"It can be done," I maintained. "With boats like these. I saw it with my own eyes, Iriti. The shallows were but a hand's breadth beneath us. But this—this lashed-together thing—still danced. Imagine what a real ship like this could do, one built by a master." I added a light seasoning of flattery.

Iriti folded his arms. "You are drunk with success. Sleep it off." His tone brooked no argument and I retreated.

The next morning, Iriti sighed when he saw me duck into his bungalow. With a wordless wave, he bade me to join him at his table. As we suckled the fat off the boar's knuckles, he finally spoke.

"This boat of yours will need more work and materials than two good canoes," Iriti began.

"I will pay you for three," I offered. Even so, Iriti looked hesitant. "And you will be forever known as the shipbuilder who conquered the Shark's Teeth."

Despite armoring his face with caution, Iriti the Older could not conceal the shine of his eyes.

THE UNUSUAL BOAT TOOK shape over the next death and rebirth of Moon. Children played in the shadow of the shipbuilder's labor, pushing their own tied-together coconut-boats into the waves in mimicry of the twin-hull design. Word spread and I found myself in dread confrontation.

"You are not crossing the Shark's Teeth," stated my mother, fanning away the noontime heat as she sat in the shelter of a mosquito net.

I grimaced, her command catching me before I could even finish sitting down across from her. Smiling uneasily, I crossed my legs and settled onto a pillow. "I will manage, mother. I am no novice wave-runner—I've been as far as the sandstone cities."

"Then make use of your experience. You've done the entire Grand Pearl," my mother said, speaking of the circular trade route connecting all the islands of the Aftersea. "Oils for Mur, black pearls for the Brae, ivory and eggs for the painted kings. You know this route well."

"Too well," I replied. "And I am not the only one. Those sea lanes are weary with boats. Every season, the prices suffer. But if I follow the sunrise, then that is something new. Unmapped lands!"

"How do you even know there is an island beyond the Shark's Teeth?" asked my mother.

"I know because they know," I said, spreading my hands upwards to where the songbirds spoke to each other above the viridian canopy. "The blue-feathers and short-beaks do not flock with the gulls. They travel alone, from island to island. When the tempests dry, we see them following the sunrise to places beyond the Shark's Teeth. You know this too, mother."

She did, but she was unconvinced. Fading hair and lined skin did not diminish her handsome features. If anything, age gave her regal gravitas. She stared at me in the manner that often sent my child-self scurrying behind a palm tree.

"All of your brothers have married," she said, beginning with a reminder that made me flinch. "The youngest Kitena girl is waiting for a good husband. You could have a bungalow, here in Ato, overlooking your father's lands. You could make a fortune with the boat you have, using the ports and contacts you know well. Why follow Sun's climb?"

"Because," I started, then stopped. My mouth worked in stupid silence. Lamely, I finished, "None of that would make me happy. Sea is calling me, mother."

To what would be my eternal surprise, my mother relented. Her shoulders sagged, almost imperceptibly, and she rotated to the side on her pillow. Her eyes closed and her chin lifted; she had always been proud. "Go, then."

I leaned forward, crossing the unseen barrier of our argument, and wrapped her shoulders with my arms.

"Visit your father before you raise your sail," she said, turning her face away.

━━━◄◆►━━━

THE GRAVE-SHRINE OF my father stood on the tallest promontory of Ato, surrounded by the embrace of cliffs. The twisting hike left me breathless; I paused to take in the roaring salt-spray of battering waves.

I knelt before all the shrines of Ato's elders, the holy men of the sixteen original families who discovered and settled these verdant shores. Their stone faces, bald and inscrutable, rose above melted candles and the skeletal remains of flowers. Solemn with respect, I prayed to Sky and Sea, to Trickster and Death, to Warrior and Mother Dirt. I even added a short utterance for the One God of the sandstone cities, for it never hurt to be inclusive in one's supplications.

The stone face representing my father gazed at me with the same stern disapproval that I remembered from him in life. My father's glare greeted me when I fell out of a banana tree after I had pelted the elder Hatano's bald head with quail eggs. His glare followed me in the aftermath of my first fermented coconut, as I dashed naked under bungalows with a piglet under one arm. He glared at me after my first failed wave-run, my canoe tattered and barely afloat.

He never lived to see me thrive, having succumbed to the wasting disease during the plague years. That did not stop me from visiting his shrine after every voyage, telling him about trades and profits, of ports new and old. I never knew whether or not he bothered to descend and listen.

On this misty morning, I found myself mute, unable to explain a plan that now seemed implausible—even to myself. I imagined his gravelly voice asking me why I was running away from being a good husband, a good son.

We scarcely talked, father and I. What I know of him I had learned from others. I confronted him about this once, jealous of my friends who all had thrilling stories of their parents' deeds during the Red Moon Wars. "The kahunas say you were a great warrior. Why haven't you told me any war stories?" my child-self demanded. "Aren't you proud to be a warrior of Ato?"

My father did not turn away from his work that morning. With great care, he had flattened and sculpted Mother Dirt so that the breadfruit trees would thrive. He said, "Boy, why should I tell you of the war? So that you can preen over the deeds of others? So that you might hate the men of Mur, whom you have not even met? Be silent and help me dig."

Chastised, I joined him and we worked together wordlessly that day and the next. He buried his past; the famed warrior spent his twilight years planting seeds for his children.

I stood and laid my hand on my father's grave-shrine. I thanked him for his guidance. Leaving the shrine, perhaps for the last time, I descended to the beach.

ATO GATHERED TO WATCH me depart. Sun had yet to bare his face. The leaves above trembled with hints of the morning wind that would guide me into warm currents. Men stood shoulder-to-shoulder with me as we pushed the unusual boat over oiled logs and into the waves.

The ocean was holy with floating candles. I could hear the encouraging shouts of children running along the beach. Women occupied the tree line, some with a babe in arm, fanning themselves with fern leaves.

I stood on the deck of the frame that bound together twin, narrow hulls, and I marveled at Iriti's work. My hands worked rope and mast with intimate familiarity. When the sail billowed auspiciously, a thrilled cry arose from the shore. I knew that if I turned my head, I would see the many and comforting faces of kin and friends, eyes bright with morning. I did not do so, for fear that such a sight would steal away my resolve.

Instead, I took the rudder and steered my ship towards untrod waves. The eyes of my people were on my back, better than any wind, and I dove into the horizon.

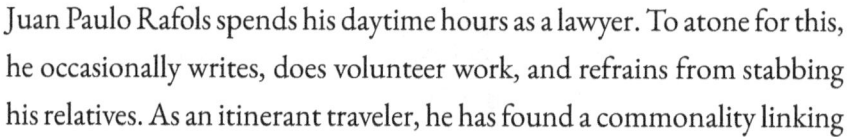

Juan Paulo Rafols spends his daytime hours as a lawyer. To atone for this, he occasionally writes, does volunteer work, and refrains from stabbing his relatives. As an itinerant traveler, he has found a commonality linking all locations. No matter where you go, you can always carry a book with you.

The Sea Witch

Shona V. Jamadi-Jaang

SY WAS A RASTAMAN WHO lived on the beach part-time, in a makeshift hut in the village of Esther along the northwest coast of Jamaica. His mother, Miss Edna, lived in the village itself.

"Sy," Miss Edna would say whenever she had the chance, "is my pride and joy! A comfort in my old age. He is a good son."

Many in the village had heard this song sung many times by Miss Edna, and they would look at Miss Edna and nod in agreement to her face. Behind her back, they would laugh and remark on the fact that, by most estimation, he had not really achieved anything significant in his thirty years on this earth, except the fact that he was a good fisherman, and the "daddy of too many chil'ren by too many women."

Still, in all his searching for love, he had yet to find his soul woman, heart, and real love.

"The seas are my love," he would tell his friends in a somewhat grandiose manner. "The wind, the sand, the call of the seagulls, the way the sun sparkle on the scales of the fish as me pull my nets in from those beautiful deep blue-grey waters. There is nothing that lift my spirits like being out there on me boat with the waters swirling around me. Ah just can't explain how Ah feel. But is something that touch me down deep."

Miss Edna never understood her son. He had been drawn to the ocean from the first time she took him there—just to look at it.

"Sy took off running like the sea was him long lost friend. He ran right into the water with me screaming at him to come back. There he was, wet an' laughin', an' there Ah was ready to beat him silly. But from that day, he always said he was goin' be a fisherman. An' as soon as he could, he would be off in that little boat an' gone for hours alone."

Miss Edna never loved the sea. The sea was just too unpredictable and mysterious. There were too many stories about how treacherous the sea could be. But Sy knew his mother loved him fiercely, and she never stood for anyone bad-mouthing him in any way. She always came to his defense. Sometimes the sea was too rough for him to stay in his hut. He would head to his mother's house and sleep in a real bed in his boyhood room.

"Aw, my little boy," she would say to him even when he was past the age when one should call a man a child, "you will always be my little boy. But one day, I hope you can settle down. All this confusion in your life cannot lead to any good, my son. Living in a hut on the beach is no kind of life. Maybe you should think about leaving the village. It would break my heart, but there's nothing much here for you to do. Jamaica has so many other places where you might be able to make a better life. What will you do when you get old?"

"Ma, I know all of these things," Sy would reply, "but let life happen in its own time. Maybe I'll go one day, and maybe it's just for me to stay and be a simple fisherman. Not everyone is made for great things."

Miss Edna would sigh and leave the matter alone. Sy would sit and eat his food as if he had not a care or a worry.

Sy's father lived in the village as well, but he had another family. Sy was the result of a passionate interlude that lasted but a minute. His father had fathered him and then went on to marry another woman from the village, and Miss Edna had spent her life, from sixteen years old onwards, trying to hide from the shame that still yapped at her heels like a pesky little dog. Sy's father acknowledged his presence and his paternity, but that was the extent of his attempts at fatherhood. He had never spent any time with Sy and until Sy turned sixteen, he merely sent a few dollars to Miss Edna by whatever missive he seemed to scrounge up. Some were not entirely honest, and sometimes money was siphoned off his meager offerings before it made its way down from his farm in the hills. At sixteen, the contributions to Sy's care stopped, as did all contact with his father who would pass him by without even a backward glance.

Sy compensated for the lack of a father by becoming a father to many—thirteen to be exact—none of whom he had the funds to provide for, and all of whom were by a total of four women. He alternated between them all for a few years before they all tired of his unexplained absences. Soon, they tired of meeting each other in the village with babies of around the same age and who looked so much like their father. Although Sy never denied his children, he spent most of his time avoiding all the mothers. But when the mothers did find him, they knew he would have nothing much to offer except fresh fish. After a while, the women stopped coming to look for him and formed a common bond, a sisterhood. Sy's Baby Mamas united in their irritation with him as a father. All except for baby number thirteen.

Baby number thirteen was called Rose, and her mother had been more than just an alternation.

"Hyacinth," Sy would become melancholy whenever he brought up the subject of Rose's mother, "she was a beauty. Rose look just like her. Now, there was a woman who Ah felt was special. Ah never will touch skin so smooth and sweet like cocoa tea with a smile that could put any sea nymph to shame!"

He had actually spent some time with Hyacinth, real passionate, lying on the beach making love in the gentle waves. Sadly, Hyacinth was very, very fragile, and even though she was eighteen years old when Rose was birthed, she had not been strong enough for the delivery.

"Ah was at her side when she passed, and Ah helped them take Rose out of her mother when she got stuck on her travels down the birth canal." His voice was heavy with a sadness that many were unaccustomed to seeing in him. Hyacinth's mother took Rose, but she allowed Sy to see her, although she expected nothing much from him and secretly blamed him for the loss of her daughter. She was gracious nonetheless.

"Sy, Ah truly believe it's a sin to keep a father away from his child—even if the father is good at making babies but not so good at taking care of their upkeep. Ah will let you come an' see Rose, an' take her to see Miss Edna. But, listen to me good! You can never take her to the sea with you, Sy." Miss Theresa's voice was firm. "She is a baby, and the sea is not safe."

"She'll be safe with me. Ah know the sea, Ma T.," he said, lifting Rose above his head as she gurgled and giggled, her blue eyes dancing.

"Absolutely not!" Miss Theresa retorted with her hands on thick hips, "If Ah ever so much as hear a rumor you have this child anywhere near a boat, Ah will never, an' mark my words, never allow you to see her again. To your mother's yard an' back again is as far as she goes. Do you hear me, Sy?"

Sy would laugh and tell her not to worry; perhaps he could take Rose when she was older.

"Perhaps no such thing," Miss Theresa would reply, and then, because she had had enough, she would declare the visit ended. Sy kissed his child and would leave them alone until another week went by and it was time for another visit.

Sy was the village bad boy. His long dreads streamed down his back. He had flawless dark skin like his mother. He was slender like her—tall and sinewy. But it was his eyes that held your attention. They were large and blue, like the ocean, a throw-back to a distant slave master. A black man with striking blue eyes was such a rarity, it gave him an almost God-like presence. He managed to get away with so much more than many males would have even dared to devise in the privacy of their thoughts. Rose had his eyes and his color. She was beautiful like her mother. But it was her eyes the villagers considered to be a definite bonus.

It was the early 1950s. The island stumbled along tightly gripped by the colonial culture which seeped over from England. Miss Theresa, Rose's grandmother, was so protective of her Rose was almost glued to her side.

"There is nothing Ah wouldn't do for this chil'. Nothin' bad will ever grace Rose's path. Ah will make sure of that. Ah lost one chil', an' Ah refuse to lose another to any errant man-child," she told Miss Edna on one of the occasions when she came by to see Rose. "Ah dare even the Almighty to come and trouble this child."

Miss Edna felt a twinge of guilt. She knew Sy had been reckless in his dealings with women.

"Yes," she said in an attempt to console Miss Theresa. "Hyacinth was much loved." But she would never admit anything to Miss T., and the conversation would take a turn down a different road.

All his life, Sy had heard of a beautiful sea woman who would come to shore around midnight, but only when the moon was big and round and shone a path along the ocean which she used to find her way. He thought it was a mountain of nonsense—old people's talk. But Sy was a romantic deep in his heart, and sometimes when he would sit on the beach—all on his own—he would stare out into the far beyond and wonder.

Fisherman talk claimed, "She is so beautiful that if a man look on her, he lose his sight. Her beauty is overpowering. There is plenty man along the coast without sight because they had the misfortune of being enchanted by her."

"You don't know! Man, she a sea-witch. Cho! She follow that moon path, an' you so busy wondering what she is that when she rise up in front of you, she catch you by surprise. You look into those sea-green eyes she have an' all this light just flash like lightning from them. You can't take her in for a long time. Your eyes not strong enough. An' if you keep trying to see what she is like behind the blinding light, all that happens is you go blind. Is true! Ah know a man down Black River way who it happened to. Blind! Can't see nothing. Have a little boy now that goes with him here an' there with a tin cup so he can beg for money since he can't go out to sea no more. All you hear when him coming is the tap-tap-tap of him cane. Sad, for true. An' he is not the only one. My father would tell me all kinds of things 'bout her an' what she did back in his day an' before."

"Cho, rubbish!" Sy would say, "No such thing. Now, Ah know Ah can let my imagination run wild like a crazed mule, but you know Jamaica is just full of old stories. Next thing you know, you going to tell me Anansi is a real man an' not a spider in a folk story."

"Eh, eh, Ah wouldn't doubt it too much either," his friend said with a serious look. "Life is a full mystery box. Who knows what happens when you remove the lid?"

Sy rolled his eyes, tossed, his locks, and went for a dip in the sea.

It was a few nights after this conversation that Sy fell fast asleep on the beach. The sound of the waves was gentle—wispy waves fingering the shore while whispering winds tickled the sands. He lay out of the tide's reach on a blanket and let the melodies of the night and the canopy of stars above lull him to sleep. A big and bright moon beamed down with benevolence. He had covered his body with the juice of a local herb, and the mosquitos kept their distance.

In his dreams, Hyacinth was on the beach. They were making love and a wave washed over them ever so carefully. His hands felt the warmth of her skin. He could feel her wet tongue in his ear and the heat as he let his hands wander over and then between her smooth thighs. He moaned happily. Knowing it was a dream, he began to open his eyes with the thought in mind that it was probably best to sleep in his hut, after all. One's back could only take lying on the sand for so long. But Hyacinth was not leaving. Her body felt solid wrapped in his embrace. His eyes flew open, and to his fright he found himself staring into the most brilliant green he had ever seen.

"What the devil..." he tried to get the words out, but soft lips tasting of salt began kissing him all over his face. Long, wet hair heavy with the scent of the ocean fell onto his face, neck, and chest. His breath stopped. He could not take his eyes away from hers until finally he found the strength to push her away.

She rolled away from him laughing—a high laugh—like some exotic sea bird.

"Don't run away," she sang as he jumped up, and he started to run. Sy was prepared to keep running when his curiosity overtook his common sense. He stopped and turned to look. The moonlight framed her as she slowly rose and, standing, looked at him, too. There was no blinding light. She took a step towards him.

"No, don't come too close. Stay where you are." He could clearly see the fineness of her face, the curve of her cheek, and the cupid's bows that were her lips. She wore a dress of delicate silver netting which left nothing hidden, and her skin was a deep copper. She was the most exquisite thing he had ever seen.

"You have ocean eyes," she said, coming towards him.

"Are you a ghost?" he asked, his voice trembling. No strength of will could steady it.

"Do I feel like one?" she replied, "You are beautiful! Your hair, your eyes... You are... different."

"You didn't kill me." Sy wished his body would respond to the danger signals his brain was sending. He could not decide whether he was incapable of moving or whether he just did not want to move. She laughed again.

That night, the beginning of their first meeting, would not be their last. So long as the moon was full for its three days of the month, Sy would make his way to the beach. He would fall asleep and she would awaken him, and they would make sweet love in the cool night sands. She told him, "Beloved, you can never see me first when I come out of the sea. I am too bright and not made for the eyes of man. It would be death for you. I will come to you first. But you must always wait for me. Never try to find me; I will always find you here. You hear the songs of the sea. They are my songs. I will always sing for you."

So Sy would lie down on the sands, and he would feel her body on his soon after he drifted off. He came even when the winds became colder, addicted to her.

Miss Theresa was not pleased that the week of the month when the moon was full he did not come to see Rose.

"Ah have been very tired these days," he told her, but he was not his usual self. His voice sounded too humble. "Ah promise to come next week an' get her. Kiss her for me."

"But she's asking for you! To her a week is a year." Her voice rose in disbelief. "Usually, Ah can't make you leave my house fast enough because you never want to leave her. You used to come around so much, an' now you hardly show up even when you supposed to. What? You have a new woman now, an' you don't have no time for your daughter? Sy, will you ever change?" She had no clue how close she was to the truth.

"Ah promise, Miss T, next week." And before she could say another word, Sy had already began to walk off. She was left standing in the middle of the street where she had happened to bump into him on her way to get Rose from nursery school.

Miss Theresa went to complain to his mother, who in turn voiced her concern because Sy was losing weight he could not afford to lose since he was so slim already.

"Something is going on with him," Miss Edna confided in Miss Theresa. "When he is not at the beach, he sleep at mine. But he is too quiet, an' spends his time drawing the phases of the moon. But he will never tell me what it for. Just mumble something about fishing and more fish come out at night. Every now and then he comes home with fish, but not like he used to; just enough for himself to eat but no extras to earn a few shillings. Ah try my best to talk to him. At nights Ah can hear him moaning an' crying in his sleep."

After many nights of this, she made him tell her what was going on and heard his story of the woman whom he went to see on the beach—the woman who only came to the beach during a full moon. She was horrified.

"Sy, my chil', this is not good. Ah begging you, Sy, stop seeing the creature 'cause in the end the only outcome of an affair with a witch is doom."

Sy would promise her, then make nightly disappearing acts. Unable to keep her concern to herself, she broke down and sent a message to Sy's father. If the man could show some interest in her son now, it might bring him back to his senses.

When Sy's father did not respond to her message, she went to the farm in person to beg Alfred to come and talk to Sy.

"He is your son. Maybe when he was younger, Ah was enough. But he needs you, Alfred. Please come an' talk some sense into your son's head. He starting to look like Death himself. Ah can't lose my one an' only chil'."

Alfred's wife, being of a good heart, felt sorry for her and forced Alfred to go and see his oldest son.

The reunion between the two was not the warm and tear-jerking encounter one might have imagined on the silver screen. Jamaican men have no time for those displays.

Alfred said, "Stop being a damn fool, boy! What you expect to come of all this? You are sleeping with the devil, an' you are on your way to hell!"

Pretty cut and dried. And with that, he went on back up the hill to the farm on his little white donkey, Burrell.

But the fact was he had even taken a few minutes to acknowledge Sy's dilemma and came as close as he possibly could to calling him "son"—"boy" would have to do. The brief visit helped Sy's brain fog to lift. Well, it began to lift. No one gets cured that fast. With a heart full of cold dread, he realized what he had been playing with—a witch from the depths of the sea. He moved back into his mother's house, abandoned his hut, and avoided the beach and the sea. When there was a full moon, Sy would not even go outside his mother's house. To him, the moon no longer signified love; it signified all the strange creatures that were supernatural in nature.

Months went by, and then years, during which time he regained his weight and began to think that the whole thing was just a hallucination.

"Sea witch!" he scoffed, "More like too much ganja!" And people would laugh and tell him, "Yes, your mind can play tricks on you."

Life in the village of Esther plodded along surefooted and without pretense. His other children grew and came to see him; some called him "Daddy." Some called him "Sy." Some did not bother to call him anything at all. But he never denied his paternity, and since he was now growing yams on a piece of land his father grudgingly gave to him, he had a little bit of stock to sell in the market. He would send a few schillings to each of his baby mamas when he could. He met a woman with a heart-shaped face and pearly white teeth who was new to the village, and who accepted his past and all the gossip that came trailing along with it. She, too, laughed at the story of the sea witch.

"You must have had a nervous breakdown," Adele reassured him, "It happened to an uncle of mine. But good food an' good thoughts can heal a sad mind."

He visited Rose on her seventh birthday. The day was so sweet Sy decided that he would take her to the beach so she could see the moon on the water for the very first time. It was his mother's turn to keep Rose overnight.

"Ma, Ah taking Rose over to Adele's house," he informed his mother. Sy had other plans, in reality. He fully intended to do this after showing Rose the moon on the water. It was dark and few people were about. He wasn't worried. Only those who had business with the sea walked the way they walked, and it was too late for fishermen to be out.

Rose was excited. She had never been out in the dark walking under the moon, and to her everything was like magic. Fireflies lit their way, owls hooted, and creatures scurried until they got to the sandy beach. It was the most astonishing sight Rose had ever seen. The moon seemed to make a road of light right through the dark water. Sy sighed in contentment as he found them a place on the sand out of the tide's reach. The salty smell of the ocean was strong. The waves made rippling and gushing noises as they touched the sands. A canopy of a trillion stars glimmered overhead.

"Baby." He cuddled his daughter as they sat on the sand. "Ah almost forgot just how peaceful and glorious this all felt."

He lay back, letting his head rest in the cool sand. Rose lay down on her back, smoothing her pretty pink dress so it covered her legs like the little lady she was, and they both looked up at the stars. The breezes sang ancient songs of the night sea. Slowly, slowly, their eyelids grew heavy.

In a panic, Sy's eyes opened as if they were on springs. Something was not right. He felt beside him. Rose was not there. He jumped up and called her name. She did not answer. The sea was no longer gentle. The waves were swelling. He raced to the water's edge, and then went in up to his waist, calling her name over and over again. From the distance, a laugh carried on the winds—a laugh that was high like some exotic seabird.

"Rose!" he screamed across the winds, but the seas merely settled once again, and the waters became calm.

Shona V. Jamadi-Jaang is a high school language arts teacher in East Anglia, UK, where she lives with her husband, Lamin, and two dogs. She has been writing since the age of six, and plans to continue as long as possible. She has a BA in English, an MS in Education, and an MA in Creative Writing. Her plan is to complete a book of short stories.

The Girl Who Wandered

Sharmaine Ford

ONCE UPON A TIME, THERE was a girl. . . Well, in these stories, there is always a girl. And usually, she is the fairest in the land. Or the cleverest. Or even just the kindest. But really, in many ways, this particular girl was like any other. Pleasant to look upon, but not beautiful. Yes, she was fairly well-mannered and kind-hearted. But, it must be said, there was a contrary streak deep down in her heart. So there were times when she may have been less than kind, occasions when she misbehaved, and every now and then—not too often, mind—she caused the villagers to roll their eyes and pity whichever fool man might take her as a wife.

However, she certainly didn't lack for young men wishing for her hand in marriage. It became almost a sport amongst some of the less genuine-hearted men, vying to see which man might bring her to heel. And she did prove to be awfully hard to pin down. Every suitor who came to her was greeted by a friendly, charming smile... Then refused on some flimsy reason. No man was quite perfect enough for her, and it seemed that even a fabled Prince Charming would fail to turn her head.

It wasn't really that she was seeking the perfect man at all. Sure, sometimes she thought it would be quite lovely to settle into the quiet stupor of love and domesticity. How simple it would be! But as the other young women around her married their sweethearts and began raising their little families, the contrary streak deep within her heart twisted, and she began to wonder. Was that all her life was meant to be? Or was there more out there, just around the corner, waiting for her to listen to that contrary streak and risk stepping around that very corner?

The heart, of all things, cannot be ignored for long. And her heart was yearning, struggling against the constraints of her life, and the narrow role she was meant to play in it. And the day came when she could remain no longer. She cast one last loving, sorrowful glance over all that had been her life, then slipped away into the shadows. So quietly she disappeared, none may notice her leaving for some days. Then, perhaps, they might grieve for her absence. But it was how it should be—following her heart into the unknown.

Two paths led from the village, winding in different directions. One led to the next town, which she had visited before, and which seemed to be a larger version of the village she was leaving. The other path, as is the way in these stories, led deep into the heart of the darkest forest. This was the path she chose.

FOR A WHILE, HER PATH was clear, and the forest was so lovely that she wondered why she had never come this way before. But as she continued through, the forest darkened, closing out the sunlight. Thorns and twigs began to tear at her skirts. The path was uneven under her feet, threatening to trip her. Every night she sought out a safe place and tried to sleep as the forest shifted and sang with the voices of its nightly creatures.

As we all know, in these stories, the young maiden comes across something or someone in the deepest heart of the forest. And thus it was for her. Just when she felt she could go no further, she came upon a small hut nestled between the trees, perhaps once a lonely woodsman's haunt. She paused before it, wondering whether she dared to enter. But really, she had come so far she felt there could be nothing left to fear. So, with steel courage comforting her weary heart, she pushed boldly on the door which opened easily at her touch.

She stepped through warily, but no monstrous creatures rushed out at her. Nothing. It was merely a small house, perhaps a touch neglected and lonely, but certainly not fearsome. She stood hesitant for a moment longer, then helped herself to a few berries from the fruit bowl—they weren't likely to be missed—and settled in to rest after her long journey and wait to see who might live in this little house in the forest

Soon enough, she glanced out of the window and weaving through the trees—glimpses of a shaggy body. Pointed ears and pointed teeth. Great wild eyes. It was heading for the small house. She bit back a gasp, her eyes darting to the fruit bowl—though why a creature with such teeth would miss a few berries, let alone have a fruit bowl, she could not fathom—and ducked behind the dusty old armchair by the fireplace. Then realised she could have slipped out the back door unseen. But too late. The front door opened and in came the Wolf.

She trembled behind the armchair. Her long journey through the forest would end here, torn to shreds to fill the belly of the Wolf. She cast her eye about, looking for some weapon—she would not be consumed without a fight!—but a sorrowful sigh caught her ear and her heart, and she peered out from behind the chair. The fearsome wolf had such a lonely look in his eyes that her heart melted. Though she shivered with fear, she slowly rose to her feet.

The Wolf stared at the Maiden with no small measure of surprise, while his heart started beating quite funnily inside his furry chest. It could easily be said that he was besotted. True, she was not the most beautiful of maidens—any hint of prettiness hidden beneath the dirt smudged on her cheeks—with her dress torn near to shreds and her hair a tangle of twigs and knots. But perhaps the Wolf recognised a streak of his own wildish nature in her heart. Or perhaps he was even lonelier than she thought. In a fairy tale—even one such as this—love cannot be realised simply by walking through one's own door. But the Wolf was yet to learn that and was very much pleased by this sudden development.

The Maiden herself was quite oblivious and was merely pleased that the Wolf was not going to eat her. In fact, he invited her to stay in his little house for as long as she wanted. The Wolf turned out to be a wonderful companion. They ran and hunted in the forest together, and the Wolf showed with her the most secret, beautiful hideaways. She did such things that would have been frowned upon in her village for a woman of her age, climbing trees, swimming in the cool river water naked, and play-fighting and laughing with the Wolf. Every night she would curl up next to the Wolf before the hearth, warmed by his thick fur, unaware of the feelings glowing in his heart.

The Wolf's love for her was such that it could not be hidden away forever. What true love deserves to be secreted away, denying the chance to shine and grow? Thus came the day when he looked over at her, seated on the bank of the river weaving daisy chains, and was so taken with love that he. It merely seemed that love meant marriage to a human woman, so that was what he suggested.

She panicked and her heart started racing around. It was true that she enjoyed the Wolf's companionship and cared for him deeply. But... Was it not this very thing that she had left her village to avoid? She could not—would not!—be tied down in such a way. No, not her. Even as she demurred from answering and sweetly kissed his dear nose—for she was so very fond of him—that contrary streak deep within in her twisted once more.

She could not bear to see the look in the Wolf's eyes when she must turn him down, so instead, she waited until he slept deeply, and then slipped away. It was the most cowardly thing she had ever done, and she could barely name the emotion that caused the tears to flow down her cheeks as she disappeared into the forest, never to see the Wolf again. And it seemed that the forest itself turned against her, tripping her up out of spite, weaving shadows around her until she was utterly lost, alone, and heart-sick.

BUT SOMEHOW, EVEN THROUGH the shadows, she managed to continue on until she stumbled into a village even smaller and more isolated than the one she had first left. She had come full circle, but she herself was changed. In her heart. In her spirit. But the villagers only saw a strange, wild woman of dirt and tears and ragged clothes. As the villagers stared in fear and disgust, she almost went straight back into the forest after spending a few coins on some bread. But she heard a whisper, a muttering, that interested her very much, and her curiosity sharpened and prickled.

For a few young village boys passed her as she sat and rested. She ignored their taunts and jibes—what did the thoughts of children matter to her?—and they soon forgot her, instead trading boasts and dares. Foolish boy talk, for the most part. But her attention was soon caught when their banter shifted to a haunted castle, long abandoned to the forest. After all, what is a fairy tale without a castle? And she knew that she wanted to find this castle, scare away whatever ghosts might linger, and make it her own.

So she stayed in the village a few more days, playing the part of a simple-minded beggar-woman while she waited and listened, piecing together the story. It had lain neglected for many generations since the Lord of the castle went insane and murdered his wife and three daughters before taking his own life. The tragedy was such that many of the older villagers refused to speak of it, and it was believed that the victims' wraiths yet haunted the castle, trailing blood through the room as they paced and wept with anguish. The story left a shiver in the young woman's heart. What a lonely existence, she thought, if indeed it was true. It steeled her resolve to find the castle. Her chance came when she happened upon two boys of the village, sneaking out into the forest. She quickly guessed their intentions and followed their bumbling progress. Her own footfalls were silent with the skills learned from the Wolf.

Deeper into the forest, following their boastful jibes at one another and their carefree laughter as they trampled the undergrowth, she kept close to them, silent and unnoticed. As the day wore on and the sun began to lower beyond the trees, the boys became somber, their glances uneasy, and their step more hesitant. Finally, they slowed to a stop, staring into the gloom ahead. She crept closer, trying to make out what they gazed upon. Trees. More trees—no, wait. A gleam of metal, drawing at the evening sun. And there—was that stone? The wall of the castle, obscured by the depths of the forest, gathered the shifting shadows to hide from the casual glance. She was here.

The boys did not hesitate for long. She followed them through the rusty iron gates and onto the courtyard. She paused in the shadows, staring in mounting delight at the weeds choking the crumbling old fountain, the uneven paving stones underfoot. And the castle. Oh, but there was no time to stand and admire. As the boys ascended the pitted stone steps to the entrance, she flew around the side of the sprawling castle, searching. A servants' entrance. She hurried through the door, grimacing as it protested loudly. She could hear the boys wandering through the castle and followed the noise until she judged that she was close. But not too close. Her wildish streak leapt forth once more, and she let out such a harrowing wail.

AAAAAIIIeeeooAAOOOO!

Such a wail that the castle stole it from her and sent it echoing throughout every room and every forgotten corner.

AAAIIIeeooAOOO...

A tormented wail such that even she fell back in fright. The boys froze for one long, horrible moment, their faces masks of horror. Then ran. Out the castle and far into the forest. She sat there, more than a touch startled, as silence fell upon the castle. Then she threw back her head and let out screams of laughter. Had the villagers heard her, their blood would have run cold, and they would have thought her a demoness.

Perhaps she was a demoness, she mused to herself. After all, she, an unremarkable woman from a small village, had spurned her suitors and walked off into the forest, faced the Wolf and, indeed, gained his love, and now she had a castle. Old, ruined, and neglected, but hers. Well, once she dealt with the other occupants of the castle. But that would be her next task.

For now, she had a castle to explore. Sooner or later, the occupants would appear. The castle—oh!—it was everything a wayward maiden would wish in a castle. Dark and dusty, shadowy and grim with sudden touches of light and beauty, hinting at happier times. Here a somber reception hall, imposing and forbidding. There a ballroom, long forgotten, silent where once there was music. Twisting corners, hidden alcoves. A library, the light of the rising moon flitting through the shutters, caressing faded tomes. Up spiral staircases, the dust failing to hide the beauty of the carved wood. The bedrooms. Her wildish heart chilled within her as she stepped inside.

She stood bathed in the moonlight streaming through the windows. The shutters lay ripped to pieces, stained dark like the pale walls, splashed with dark stains. Like the bed. And the floor. The whole room, washed with blood. Horror and fury mounting, she fled, footsteps echoing down the hallway to the next room. And the next. And the master bedroom. All stained with the massacre of innocents. Furious, she screamed out, seizing a broken chair—even the furniture was broken and bloodstained!—and threw it across the room. The action released emotion that words could not express. The blood! No one—not the villagers, not kin—had thought to cleanse the blood? What soul could rest when their lifeblood yet lay before them? What peace could there be for those poor haunted wraiths?

A chill spread across her skin leaving trails of goosebumps and stealing the warmth from the blood in her limbs. Her cheeks drained of colour. The wraiths. They were here, waiting for her. She stood her ground, eyes shifting around the moonlit room.

"Show yourself to me," she commanded, her voice quavering only a little. "I will not run from you. I do not fear you."

The room remained silent and empty. Then the gentle sweep of ice across her skin. A shape materialized before her. It was a pale, ghostly woman with such sorrow and fear etched on her features. Translucent blood dripped from the wounds on her body, her limbs, her face. Her hands clenched tightly to a figure behind her. A young girl, peering fearfully around her mother's skirts, blood flowing down her cheeks like tears. Two more figures slowly emerged from shadow and moonlight, clustering around the older woman. Two bloodied maidens, one barely out of childhood, the other only a handful of years younger than our heroine herself. Perhaps once this ghostly maiden had suitors of her own. Now there was nothing but death, blood, and the memory of pain. The last whisper of fear left the living, beating heart of the wandering maiden, leaving only such sorrow for their tragedy.

She gazed upon the wraiths with such compassion, from the very depths of her strong, rebellious heart.

"I will try to give you the peace and rest you deserve," she said, her voice soft. A glimpse of hope caught in the mother's eyes, quickly replaced with wariness. The Maiden continued, "I will cleanse the house of the blood of the innocents. Then you may move on into the next world. Or you may stay with me in this castle. I hope, if you choose to stay, you will come to trust me, for I cannot harm you, but nor will I run in fear."

The wariness remained in the mother's gaze, but she nodded, just once, as her middle daughter began to weep silently. Her heart resolved to her task, the wildish Maiden bowed her head to the four bloodied wraiths. She retreated from the room and made her way to a guestroom in the far wing of the castle—dusty, musty, and neglected—but unstained by blood. So late was the night, and so exhausted was she, that she fell onto the bed, not bothering to change from her ragged clothes, and fell asleep.

She awoke with the first light of the sun and rose from her dusty bed. A glance in the cracked mirror revealed a face streaked with dirt, scoured by the elements from her time in the forest. If once her plain face did not attract many compliments, now, certainly, she looked like some wildish creature. But she merely shrugged; any attractiveness in her features would make little difference to the hard work ahead. She made her way out to the forest, enjoying the sun warm upon her hair, as she foraged to break her fast. Then, determined, she set about her task collecting a bucket and water, a stout boar bristle brush, a mop, a rag to tie her hair back from her face, and her own stubborn will. And thus she began. Mopping away decades of dust in the first of the bloodstained rooms was the easy part. Then she began to scrub. And scrub. She scrubbed until her hands and knees ached, her back stiff. And then longer still. As she scrubbed, she sang softly to herself to pass the time, and occasionally she felt the chill of the ghosts' presence, though they did not show themselves to her. They merely watched as this lone maiden scrubbed away the blood that no one else had bothered with.

Finally, on the third day—or was it the fourth? Time had lost meaning while she worked—she sat back with a sigh, letting the brush fall to her side. It was done. She felt a chill on her cheek, an icy kiss.

She never saw the ghosts again, though sometimes she would feel them brush past her. Sometimes they would guide her with a flash of white, a swirl of dust, leading her to some treasure. Wardrobes of clothing barely touched by time. Storerooms where she found enough coin to live comfortably. The hidden keepsakes of the eldest daughter. In this way, she knew herself accepted in the castle. A handful of months passed idly as she took to tidying up the rest of the castle. It would never do to cast away all of its shadows.

———————◆◇◆———————

WHILE SHE KEPT TO THE castle and the surrounding forest, occasionally she would travel down to the small village. Her appearance—in clothing she found with the guidance of the ghosts, her face scrubbed clean of dirt and her hair combed reasonably tidily—was such a departure from her first visit to the village, fresh out of the wilds of the forest, that none of the villagers recognised her. And she walked with such a wildish grace and surety, and took so little notice of their stares, that their curiosity grew, wondering where this young woman had appeared from. Dressed as she was, she might even be of noble blood. And here she was, wandering the village with no male companion, and then disappearing back into the forest. They noticed her. And they wondered.

The day came that one of the boys in the village summoned up the courage to follow her as she disappeared back into the forest. By then, she had lived alone in her castle for some months, and perhaps she had lost some of her instinctive wildishness, for she did not notice her follower. Instead, she unwittingly led him right to her abode. The boy was astounded. This young woman lived in the haunted castle! What matter of woman would do so? A witch? An enchantress? Was she in fact a demoness, or a spirit? Excited and fearful, he rushed back to the village and babbled of his discovery with such feverish passion that they first thought him possessed. When they pieced together what he was saying, a shadow fell over each and every heart. For here was proof that the young woman who had appeared so suddenly was indeed a malignant being no doubt plotting their demise. For surely no innocent maiden could reside in the haunted castle.

For two nights, she continued as before, doing as she pleased in her castle and the forest surrounding it with no one but the ghosts for company. It seemed to her that they were making their presence more obvious than before, sending chills across her skin at odd moments, making her jump and frown. Were they playing with her? Warning her? Trying to scare her away? She mused it over, feeling a restlessness settle in her wildish heart. She had been here for such a time. Perhaps she was ready to move on. But she put it off, stalled, and waited. For she was quite comfortable alone with her ghostly companions in her castle.

Then, on the third night as she was readying herself for bed, she gazed out the window and a full, bright moon caught her attention. Her wildish heart twisted and leapt within her and she knew. The next day. She would leave the next day. She must leave and venture forth once again.

And she settled happily into bed, taking one slow look around her room before snuffing the candles and letting herself drift to sleep knowing that tomorrow... tomorrow...

She awoke with an ice-cold shock, as if dumped into a half-frozen pond, and shot upright, glaring around the moonlit room. What cruel trick was this for the ghosts to awaken her in such a manner? She reached out to light a candle then stopped, a chill running down her spine that for once was not the touch of the ghosts. Murmurs, voices, drifting up from the courtyard below. Quietly, quietly, she rose from her bed and crept to the shutters, easing one open just enough to peer down onto the courtyard. Her room was positioned in the east tower, with a perfect view over the courtyard from one side, and of the forest reaching up to the stone wall surrounding the castle on the other side. Her heart skipped a beat as she stared down. Shadows gathered in the courtyard, bundled together like sheep. Men, if she was not mistaken. Villagers coming to banish the ghosts of the castle. Or coming to banish her? She cursed herself for a fool ten times over, for all the days she had wasted sitting here in her castle, thinking herself safe and secure. Well, it looked like she would surely pay for it now.

Fury flared up within her, and she flung the shutter open, leaning out into the moonlit night.

"Who dares to come here?" she screamed down at the gathering figures of the villages. "Who dares to disturb me?"

The ghosts, her companions, flung her words down to the courtyard, flung them echoing through the castle, accompanied by their own anguished wails. Faces, upturned to her window, shadowed with fear. There was milling, reluctance, until one hardy soul stepped forth.

"We come for you, demoness," he bellowed, emboldened by the crowd around him. "To drive you away from our village before you wreak havoc on us."

"If she has not already," put forth another man, safely behind the first speaker.

Before she could speak further, a multitude of voices cursed her, accusing, angry. She tried screaming at them as they began to throw rocks, as they rushed toward the castle doors. Frustrated, she fell back. And if before she had cursed herself, it was nothing to the blasphemies on her tongue now. Foolish, foolish! Mere words would not turn them back. If anything, her words had roused them further. And now they knew where she was. Now, she had to leave.

Barely pausing to throw a cloak over her nightgown, she rushed out of the bedroom, down the hallway, down the stairs. Cold whispered across her skin as she went, the ghosts urging her on. She could just hear the villagers breaking into the castle, and she fled the opposite direction. Fled through a parlour, where she hesitated, before hefting up a weighty iron candelabrum. A feral smile dashed across her lips, and she carried the candelabrum with her. Voices and thundering footsteps chased her out the servants' entrance and into the gardens behind the castle, into the darkness, into the shadows.

She made her way through the overgrown garden to the small back gate set in the crumbling stone wall. Just as she laid her hand upon the cold iron, voices crashed behind her, followed by figures rushing towards the back entrance of the castle, figures forming into three men, rough village men. She froze - they froze - shadows and moonlight dancing as the world shifted, and fear spread into her very limbs. Only a moment - a lifetime - then she flung the gate open and fled into the forest as the men ran towards her.

The candelabrum was a heavyweight in her hand, slowing her down, but she did not dare cast it aside. Branches, leaves, brambles, and stones ripped at her as she ran, stumbling and gasping. Something - a stone, a root - caught against her foot, and barely cutting back a shriek, she tripped and fell to the ground, the candelabrum tumbling from her hand. She barely noticed the pain lashing her knees and palms as she pushed herself up and scrambled for her one weapon.

Footsteps crashed closer. Cursing voices were so close—right behind her, almost on top of her! Her hand wrapped around the cold iron candelabrum and she wrenched it around, swinging the heavyweight with pure desperation. It collided against a hand sweeping a wooden staff at her head; collided with such fury that the villager bellowed with pain as his staff was knocked away. He fell back, hesitating. She surged to her feet, getting tangled in her cloak, in the undergrowth, but fighting free. As she raised the candelabrum, she caught a glimpse out of the corner of her eye—two more men close behind him, and a third man sweeping out of the forest to join them.

No. No. She would not die here without a fight. As the first man regained his courage and reached towards her, sneering even through his pain, she howled at him, wordless rage, and dodged his rough hands. Swinging the candelabrum with all her weight behind it, she hit him solidly over the head. He staggered and wavered before collapsing to the ground. She staggered and almost fell herself, but she set her teeth and turned towards the other men.

Then she blinked, confused, gripping her candelabrum closer. Two of the men grappled, fighting over possession of a heavy-bladed knife, silvery in the moonlight. There had been one more. There on the ground was a shadowy lump, his face darkened with blood. Someone had already dealt with him. She moved toward the two men fighting. But which was trying to help her? As she hesitated, one man glanced toward her, taking in the two men already slumped to the ground and the weapon in her hand. Fear widened his eyes and with a cry he broke free from his assailant, relinquishing the knife, and darted back towards the castle. The other man moved as if to follow, but she called out.

"Wait! We must go! There are too many of them back there."

Was that her own voice, so strong and sure, betraying none of the fear quivering through her body?

He turned to stare at her, his face clear in the moonlight—just one moment, one glimpse which froze her tongue with bewilderment. He grasped her arm and pulled her deeper into the forest, away from the castle as if it had been his thought in the first place.

Deeper into the forest they fled, away from the castle, far from the villagers. Finally, in a small moonlit hollow, they stopped for a breath. He was restless, staring back from whence they came, as if expecting the villagers to yet follow them. She studied his face in the moonlight. Surely he was no one she had ever met before. His features brushed close to beautiful, but just fell short as if an artwork by an apprentice copied from a Master's work. Almost beautiful. Not quite human. Then he turned back to her, and looked at her as if he knew her.

His expression faltered at her confused frown. "Do you not recognise me?"

So she did know him from somewhere? "Oh! Sorry, it's been so long, I was not sure." Her voice trailed off as she searched her memory, pulling up all the faces of her spurned admirers, even her detractors from her own village, or those from the village near the castle.

His face fell even further. "You don't recognise me," he replied flatly.

Something about the way he held himself, as a being more accustomed to the forest than a village, more accustomed to running as a... No. That couldn't be.

"The Wolf!" she gasped suddenly, staring at him in shock. "But no. You're... not a wolf."

"I..." He looked away shyly. "I thought you might love me if I was human. So when you left, I... I searched for a swamp witch to turn me human so that you would love me." The last words fell out in a rush as he gazed down on her, fearful of her rejection.

"You changed into a human so that I would love you? What the hell is this, some sort of fairy tale?!"

Yes. This is a fairy tale. Things happen in fairy tales that would never, ever happen in reality. So let's just go with it, okay?

"Okay," she replied, drawing a deep breath.

"I did not run away because I did not love you," she began slowly, each word chosen carefully, "but because... because I do not wish to be a wife, to be someone's—anyone's—property. I ran away from my village to escape that fate. I want to wander and explore, love and learn. I do not wish to be shackled to one place, to one life. It is no reflection on how I feel about you, be you Wolf or man. Indeed, I am very fond of you. But that domestic life is not for me."

"Oh." The Wolf frowned into the shadows. "I thought, as a maiden, that marriage would be what you wanted. Wolves do not marry. It is a human concept. Wolves live and love and roam freely. But—" Was he blushing? "But, perhaps, if you are fond of me and I am fond of you... Perhaps we can wander together. Explore together. And love each other."

Yes, he was indeed blushing fit to brighten the night sky. "For as long as we both wish to do so. No shackles. For neither of us would do well in captivity."

She stepped forward and took his hand, kindly ignoring that in the moonlight it may have looked decidedly like a paw. "That sounds acceptable to me," she replied simply, for she was weary of all the grand words and concepts. "Though it seems that we cannot go back to the castle, so we must wander on. However—" She broke off, frowning down at the cloak covering her nightgown. "I may need to acquire some more suitable clothing."

A series of crashes came from the castle, followed by ragged cheers, and punctuated her words. It seemed the villagers wouldn't leave much left to salvage. How very inconvenient.

THEY HUDDLED IN THE depths of the forest for what little remained in the night. Dawn revealed the ruin of the castle, and all she had worked on for the past months was destroyed. They had little choice but to move on.

And so, they moved on after a sneaky trip into the village, where the Maiden borrowed a few clothes to replace those destroyed in the castle.

"After all," she explained, "It is recompense for the emotional trauma the villagers have put me through." With that stubborn look on her face, the Wolf wasn't about to disagree even if he was inclined to. And he was still a wolf at heart. Human morals weren't his area of expertise.

So, now properly clothed, the Maiden and the Wolf-Who-was-a-Man ventured back into the forest. Together.

In most fairy tales, perhaps, I would go on to say that they lived happily ever after. But I cannot, for I do not myself know that this is so. But the last I saw of them, they did seem happy enough, traipsing around on more adventures than I could possibly describe. You would have to ask them yourselves, if you ever see them. You will recognise them if you do. The Maiden with a pleasant smile and a wildish glint in her eye, and the Man who yet walks with a Wolfish stride.

Sharmaine Ford lives in New Zealand. Her stories are a mixture of gothic and fairy tales. Her love for the world of fantasy began at 12, when she read the Redwall series. Once she hit high school, she stepped into the adult world of fantasy. Like most with a passion for the genre, Sharmaine wanted to live in a fantasy world.

Sammna and Porridge

Penny Westhorp

SAMMNA STOOD ON A HILL overlooking the wall that separated the Female Enclave from the Male Enclave. Usually, she was fascinated by the mysterious male area, but today she ignored their land. She strained to see the small blue V of ocean, visible between the folds of hills. At her side, her pet emcrit Porridge morphed to look like an eagle, its eyes fierce and sharp. The sea was the most exciting thing Sammna knew of—changeable but always there, promising adventure far away but always returning to shore. Today, however, the thick humid air obscured that tantalising glimpse.

She folded her arms around her skinny frame and then, irritated by the feel of her breasts, dropped them again. Ever since her body had started changing, her discomfort about who she was had intensified. She had always been unsure, but now she felt wrong somehow. As her frustration rose, the emcrit shaded into a cranky hen, scolding and ruffling its feathers. She reached down and smoothed its raised crest. Sammna sighed, releasing her irritation, and Porridge soothed into its natural shape. Its colourless fur lay shining and sleek along its back. It stood a little below her knee height. Porridge folded its six stubby legs under its long soft body and tucked its blunt nose into its chest. Soft snores whiffled the fur.

"Come on," Sammna urged the somnolent beast as she turned away from the wall and began the long walk back up the road to the Core of the Female Enclave. "Hurry up, Porridge. I can't be late for Temple." Porridge looked up uncertainly. "It's the memorial for our escape from the plague. You remember." The emcrit shook its head. "No, you wouldn't, I suppose. 'The annual ceremony to celebrate the eradication of the heterosexually transmitted plague and the founding of the Enclave system which saved humanity,'" she recited. "I don't know how many centuries ago, but you'd think they'd be over it by now." Porridge reflected her bored mood by making itself pale grey all over, and trundled after her.

She looked back toward the now invisible ocean. "I might have a chance to go to the seaside if I could become male. And that's not going to happen anytime soon."

Porridge nodded and grew an appendage that looked like a little furry penis between its last pair of legs. It rolled over, waving its limbs, and she laughed with genuine amusement.

"I wish I could become a boy that easily!" The emcrit reverted to its own shape. "But surely there's more to being a man than just that?" Porridge shrugged. As Sammna had done many times before, she shrugged too, a deep rolling motion, wishing she could morph like Porridge into a body that felt like it fitted.

Her mouth sagged open as she considered what she'd said. Goosebumps prickled down her arm. Something was ringing true inside her. She was meant to be male. The revelation stunned her so much that she sat down suddenly beside the road. Porridge crouched beside her, crooning worry. She should have been a boy! Able to do all the things boys could do! The thought made her head whirl. Porridge shaped into a little boy with her features. She smiled and scratched its head. Mouth gaping in the caricature of elation, the little boy hopped and twirled out onto the path. She grinned, watching as it became more animated the more excited she felt.

After a few moments, she took a deep breath. Time to get her thoughts—and more importantly, her feelings—under control. It wouldn't take much for others to guess this shattering revelation if the emcrit was walking around looking like a small male version of herself.

Sometimes she almost regretted having impressed the little creature. She'd never thought it would be possible to be sorry about that. She had been only nine years old at the time, and had ignored the warnings of her older Sisters. How could having a pet for life, one who understood your every feeling, be a bad thing?

Gazing at her newly-impressed pet, she had continued to stroke the soft fur, marvelling as it reflected the colour of her hand with each pass. An emcrit was every child's desire, wasn't it? And she was so lucky to have come across its nest on her solitary ramble through the scrublands. They were very rare, she knew. And the babies were only impressionable for such a short time. To have discovered one unguarded was a sign. A sign that she should take it and bond with it and never feel alone again. Ever. It would stay with her for the entire length of her life. She had heard a terrible story of a woman who had killed her emcrit to be free of the demands of the bond. She couldn't understand how the woman could do such a thing. Never! She would never, ever commit such a horrendous heartless act.

Now, Sammna shook her head as she walked back toward home. She loved her unusual pet. It aroused curiosity wherever she went. As far as she knew, there was only one other in the entire Female Enclave, enmeshed with a girl in the last years of her Acolyteship. Bonding with an emcrit had certainly changed Sammna's life. She had learned very quickly to mask her feelings, not only from others around her, but almost from herself. If she allowed herself to experience any strong emotion, it showed immediately in the emcrit's form. Sometimes the embodiment of her moods was so funny that it made her laugh, effectively changing the emotional state, so that the creature morphed back into its own shape. She needed to do that now.

She straightened her back, gazing up at the looming grey stone bulk of the Goddess's Temple as it appeared over the crest of the hill. Squatting like a great toad in the centre of the Core, it was a troubling symbol in her life. What would the Temple Mistresses think about her feeling she should have been born male? Porridge was flipping between a representation of the statue of the benign Goddess, and a caricature of the Most Elder Sister in her formal robes, frowning and shaking her finger. Sammna laughed, breaking the morph, and stilled her mind. The emcrit shrank back into its natural flowing form and paced beside her.

That night in bed, she lay awake, keeping very still so as not to disturb her roommates, Elliane and Janess. She was too busy thinking to sleep. I feel like a boy trapped in a girl's body. The thought would not leave her mind. Luckily Porridge was asleep in its pouch, hung in the wardrobe, or it'd be bouncing around the room as a male. Her mind moved in slow circles to a truly radical notion: might it be possible to become a boy? The idea shocked her. She didn't know how it could happen, but it seemed like such a good—no, a necessary—thing to do.

She lay straight, thinking and staring at the ceiling, her hands pushing her small breasts flat. It was something she had started doing as they had developed. She had a constant sense that something was wrong with her, that she looked bizarre even though she looked like everyone else. She hated the idea of her breasts, pushing her out of shape. So she had trained herself to sleep either on her stomach to squash them, or to keep pressing them with her hands. A new aspect worried her: If she were to become a boy, what could she do about her figure? And worse than that, where would she live? It would mean she had to leave the Female Enclave. No one ever did, except for those who suffered the most severe punishment of Expulsion. Becoming a boy would surely be serious enough to warrant that!

Just thinking about the Expelled gave her the shivers. Everyone knew that the Expelled was populated by damaged, malevolent people who hated the Enclaves. That was why Expulsion was the worst punishment the governing Council of Mistresses could inflict.

But perhaps, rather than waiting for Expulsion, she could dress up as a boy, and hide her breasts somehow, and go live in the Male Enclave? She grimaced to herself. How stupid. How would she ever get out of the Female Enclave without the Protectors noticing?

The whole next week was devoted to preparing for Summer Festival. It was the biggest event of the year. Every woman looked forward to at least some part of the annual fertility rites. There would be men coming into the Enclave and participating in the formal religious blessing in the Temple. And then for the Acolytes, the best part: the Fair with all the year's production on sale, and there would be bands and dancing. Later, the adult women could choose a man to lie within the Summer Field. That last thought made her intensely uncomfortable.

Everyone participated in the preparations. She was part of the team building the stalls and trestles for the Fair. Sammna didn't mind this physical work of readying the area for the fun part of the evening. She hadn't wanted to go with Ellianne, who had been sent off with Tomma, one of their neighbours on the First's floor of the Acolytes Hall. They were to shepherd the sheep that were cropping the grasslands between the Wall and the Core to a short turf, readying for the night of procreation. Just the thought of all that sex was enough to make Sammna feel very uptight. Janess had volunteered to be one of those staying behind and minding the children so the usual carers could participate in the Festival. She was going with Rosie, who shared with Tomma and Gaia next door.

Sammna felt excitement squirming in her stomach. She would see men and boys again, for only the second time in her life. This year she wouldn't be part of the incoming ceremony. That was reserved for the newest Firsts. As a second-year First, she would be part of the crowd of waiting women lining the processional route.

She remembered how strange it had been last year, when she and Ellianne and Janess—along with all the other newly initiated Firsts—had dressed in the pastel robes reserved for the acolytes who were permitted to witness only the opening ceremonies. They were too young to be allowed to go the field with the men. They had lined the processional route with their flaming torches, ushering the incoming males to the great ritual in the Temple. The witnessing boys had been interspersed in their line. For the first time ever, she had stood shoulder to shoulder with strangers of the opposite sex. And later, they were going to dance with the boys! Her arm holding the torch had shaken with the immensity and intensity of her feelings. The excitement, the anticipation, and the curiosity were so strong she could barely look at them.

This year though, all through the night of Summer Festival, Sammna watched the boys and men. She had left Porridge tucked up in their room in the Acolytes Hall. She shook her head at the idea of bring the emcrit to the Fair. She'd seen what happened to the other girl who had displayed her pet last year. Men and boys had mobbed around her until her emcrit had morphed into an uncontrollable lion cub, scratching and screeching and spitting at anyone reaching towards it. Apparently, the men had never seen anything like it. She had heard them say that there were no emcrits in the Male Enclave. It had puzzled her why not. Was the land or the climate somehow different there? Could men not impress emcrits? She had wondered for a long time after last year's event.

Anyway, tonight she could think about what it might be like to be a boy without Porridge giving her away. The older men were too different to even contemplate. But the boys... surreptitiously, she practiced walking with their lengthened stride, bouncing slightly on the balls of her feet. She saw the way they slouched, and the way they sat with their elbows resting on their splayed legs. She was as tall as most of them, and their hair was similar to girls'. For a couple of hours, she observed, rehearsed, and dreamed of what life would be like if only she had been born a boy.

Sammna caught sight of the girls from next door, Gaia and Tomma. They were talking with a boy clutching a tankard. She wasn't sure, but from Tomma's dreamy expression it might be the boy she had met and danced with last year. Sammna stood behind a flap of canvas on the next stall and observed. She watched the way the boy moved, placed his hands, and shuffled his feet. She looked at his clothing—a long, soft, open-necked tunic tied across his hips. His trousers looked very similar to the type Sammna and all the girls wore for their defence training in the Perimeter Squad. He had boots that reached to his calf and laced around his ankles. Their cracked folds had been highly polished, presumably for tonight's occasion. He and Gaia were talking about ships and trading goods; apparently, his father was a grazier and he lived on a farm, not far from the Wall. Tomma seemed to be ignoring the conversation, and was just gazing at the boy with a slight smile as she watched his animated face. But Gaia kept asking the kinds of questions Sammna would have asked if she had been his friend, about how they shipped animals, meat, and wool through a trading company. She listened avidly. Every detail about the way boys lived was fascinating. She resolved to ask Gaia more about the Male Enclave the next day. Gaia wouldn't mind her being curious.

Late that night, Sammna watched as many of the young lads headed back to the Male Enclave. They talked and laughed, and punched each other on the shoulder, and slung their arms around a friend's neck. They trooped through the Gate, guarded by the formidable Protectors. She felt a great loss to see them go. She wouldn't be so close to boys again for a whole year.

She began walking slowly back to the Acolytes Hall, staring up at the stars. In the clear dark of the night, she stopped. Realisation crystallised within her.

I am male.

I am truly male.

Somehow I got born with the wrong body, but inside, I am a boy.

The clear starry sky, the warm balmy air, and the muted sounds from the Festival burned into her mind. I will always remember this moment, she thought, this particular moment when I knew for sure.

Sammna sat in the long grass beside the road, questions fermenting in her mind. Do I call myself he or she now? It seemed insurmountable. Thinking of herself in the past as 'she' seemed fine because she had been a girl then. But now? 'He' was what fitted best. But it wouldn't work in the exclusively Female Enclave. He would have to refer to himself as 'she' for the time being. How would other Acolytes react if they discovered she was male inside? What would happen if the Mistresses knew? She shuddered with apprehension about being found out. What changes might it make to her relationships with Janess and Ellianne? Would they still love him as a sister—no, a brother? It was so difficult to navigate the changes in pronouns, let alone gender and relationships. And what about love? It was the norm for girls to have intimate relationships with each other in the Female Enclave. Would she still desire girls? Being male would create the abnormal heterosexual dynamic. Or did she—no, he—desire men, as so many women had done this very night? It was all so confusing. It made her head hurt.

Sammna checked on Porridge when she entered their room. It was curled up in its pouch, sound asleep, shaped as a miniature boy, sucking its thumb. She grimaced. It was going to be very, very hard to keep this conviction from showing.

The next day Sammna took Porridge for a walk with Ellianne. Porridge kept morphing into a boy, despite Sammna's attempts to suppress any such thoughts.

"Why is he doing that, Sammna?" Ellianne asked.

Flustered, Sammna joked that it must be picking up her desire to see boys again at next year's Summer Festival.

"But why does it look like you? Why not like a different boy?" Ellianne asked, frowning as she picked up the miniature lad and settled him on her hip. Sammna swallowed hard.

"Umm, I suppose Porridge is using the features it knows best?" she offered. She shuddered, terrified of what would happen if Ellianne discovered her inner state.

Later that afternoon, Sammna saw Tomma and Rosie leaving their room. Taking Porridge, she went next door and knocked. Gaia let her in and seemed happy to talk about everything she had learned about men, and the Male Enclave. Sitting on Gaia's lap, Porridge morphed into a little boy with Sammna's features. Gaia stilled and looked at Sammna for a long moment.

"I think," Gaia began carefully, passing the emcrit back to her, "it must be difficult sometimes to have a pet that displays your every emotion."

Sammna gulped. Could Gaia tell what she was feeling? Could she trust Gaia with her awareness of being a boy? She opened her mouth to speak, but Gaia interrupted, "Tell me about the bond you have with Porridge. It's the most endearing little animal."

Sammna stopped. Best not to reveal her male gender, not to anyone. Instead, she talked about the consequences of impressing an emcrit: The magic of the mental bond that formed as soon as the emcrit impressed; that it lived as long as you did; if you stayed together, it died when you died; you couldn't give it away and you couldn't abandon it, as it would die a slow death of starvation and misery; you couldn't set it free in the bush—it no longer had the ability to initiate morphing to save itself from predatory animals, and it couldn't return to its species: wild emcrits would kill it because it was too alien, bonded to a human instead of to its natural morph group; it was forever dependent up on its bondmate for its physical sustenance, and for the emotional connection which made its life worth living.

"Ah," said Gaia, looking straight at Sammna, "then it really is a link you mustn't break. No one could possibly leave their emcrit, could they?"

Sammna shook her head, miserable on the horns of dilemma. If she wanted to be male, what would she do with Porridge? From then on, her daydreams became even more fraught.

———————◆O◆———————

FOR THE NEXT YEAR, Sammna schooled herself to think of nothing but her assigned work and being with her friends any time Porridge was with her. She suppressed her desire to be a boy so hard there were days when she didn't even think about it. But her dreams were always about living the life she imagined males led, full of action and adventure and choice. And more and more often, in the morning the emcrit was a little boy. She dreaded bringing Porridge out of its pouch, and started inventing reasons why she wouldn't rouse it until Janess and Ellianne had left the room.

She became convinced she couldn't go on living the way she was. She felt constantly awkward, always aware of her breasts and the confusion between being male inside, and having a female appearance. She was tense and unhappy most of the time, which Porridge reflected by slinking around looking like a wet cat. She couldn't tell anyone what was troubling her, not even Janess and Ellianne. The more imperative the idea of being male became, the more alone she felt. Even a hint that she dreamed sometimes of living in the Male Enclave would be enough to have her interrogated before the Council of Mistresses. But in secret she experimented with binding her breasts flat. She practiced walking with a longer loping gait. She deepened her voice, until it became a habit. But none of it felt enough. She could not openly approach becoming a male while she lived in the Female Enclave.

So Sammna began to work out scenarios of how she could escape. The most likely was to disguise herself as a boy. She would hide her shape under a boy's tunic. And if she was very cautious, she could probably dye her spare pair of Perimeter Squad trousers black. Her hair and boots were similar enough. Time and time again she daydreamed about going to Summer Festival, wearing a male outfit under the robe she wore every day. Then, when all the boys were streaming back to the Male Enclave, she would somehow join them, and pass through unnoticed.

"What if I really left, and lived as a boy, Porridge?" she mused one day, sitting on her bed and stroking her pet. Porridge stared at her with enormous black eyes and morphed into an emcrit corpse. Its chest caved in, the skin leathery and the tiny feet clawed. "Oh dear Goddess!" Sammna muttered. "Come back, Porridge, come back!" Porridge expanded again into its original form, but its colourless fur was lying flat and dull. It crept into the wardrobe and climbed into its pouch. When Sammna went to comfort it, Porridge was lying curled into a ball with its back to her. It refused to respond.

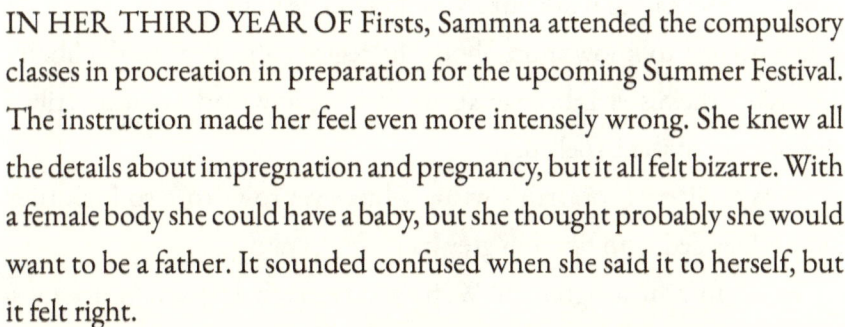

IN HER THIRD YEAR OF Firsts, Sammna attended the compulsory classes in procreation in preparation for the upcoming Summer Festival. The instruction made her feel even more intensely wrong. She knew all the details about impregnation and pregnancy, but it all felt bizarre. With a female body she could have a baby, but she thought probably she would want to be a father. It sounded confused when she said it to herself, but it felt right.

One morning, about two weeks before Summer Festival, she realised she was making actual plans to leave. She wasn't just daydreaming about it. She really was going to escape. But she could not bear the idea of the pain she would feel. What about her relationship with Ellianne and Janess? Could she abandon their friendship, their sisterhood, to realize the need to be male? But worse still, what would happen to Porridge? What could she possibly do with the emcrit? She could not take it into the Male Enclave. Emcrits didn't exist there, so she knew it would immediately mark her as female. And the alternatives were too terrible to contemplate. Stay as a girl to preserve Porridge's life, or abandon the emcrit to die in order to live true to her own nature?

Sammna tossed and turned every night. She felt nauseous all the time, and had to take time off from her student placement. And Porridge looked terrible. The little emcrit was thin and lackluster and spent most of its time looking like a sick dog. Sammna avoided looking at it, feeling too conflicted about needing to leave and wanting to find a way not to hurt it. And despite all this, the conviction in her grew that living as a male was the only way to be content within her own person.

Three days later, while washing clothes, Sammna had a wonderful idea. She could leave and take Porridge with her by going through the Male Enclave and then escaping unnoticed into the region of the Expelled. But... But... Her mind stammered with the enormity of the thought. Live in the forsaken region? All on her own—no, live as a male on his own—surrounded by the vicious, deranged Expelled? Might it be possible? She had to work out a way it could be done.

She needed to know more about the region. She went to the library and asked the Sister Librarian at the desk for any works that described the domain of the Expelled.

"Why?" Sister Librarian's wispy white eyebrows rose so high they almost blended with her thin grey hair.

"Er, it's for... an assignment. We have to research different professions. And I was given, ummm..." She struggled to think of any occupation that needed to know about the Expelled. "Um, I was given, er, the Temple

Mistresses. They need to know about the Expelled because they have to condemn women to Expulsion, right?" She looked hopefully at the librarian.

"They do not. It is the Council of Mistresses who pass sentence." The Librarian now frowned so hard her eyebrows almost obscured her pale eyes.

"Oh, that's right. I have to research the Chief Temple Mistress who sits on the Council. I always get the Council and the Temple Mistresses confused," Sammna stammered, hoping the Sister would just think her stupid and stop asking questions.

Sister Librarian gave her a slip of paper with a stack and shelf number, grumbling that the Learning Rooms should remember to let the library know about the demands for assignments.

Sammna skimmed through the text, glossing over the parts she knew—how the Enclaves had been formed hundreds of years ago, following the identification of the fatal heterosexually transmitted plague which had threatened to annihilate the entire population. She found a map of the original Enclaves and sketched a rough copy. But what fascinated her was the discovery that some people had not entered the safety of the Enclaves. They had stayed in the area now known as the Expelled.

So if they survived, they would have had children, she thought. She felt exultant. A euphoric voice within her kept chanting, 'There must be men and women together there! You could live as a man! Everyone you met would believe you were male from the very beginning.' The notion of a fresh start, where no one knew her history, glowed like a beacon.

But then the jubilation faded. Could she bear to leave everything she knew, everyone she loved and cared for, and go alone into the unknown? The idea was overwhelming. But so was the distress she was living in. Could she take Porridge into the Expelled? Sammna went back to the Librarian and asked for another reference text on the wildlife of the region. She endured the grumbles and raised eyebrows without much concern. But she could find no references to emcrits—either wild or bonded—in the Expelled.

For the next week, she endured the daily routines feeling as though she was sequestered behind glass. She could hear and see, but things didn't seem to touch her. She went through the motions of sharing everyday activities with Ellianne and Janess. She attended class but nothing stuck in her mind. As her internal world became consumed with the idea of leaving, she looked at her friends, teachers, workmates, and fellow Firsts with a muted curiosity. This was the last time she would ever see them. She would never know how this girl turned out, or what would happen to that Mistress. This was the last time she'd go to the Temple. She used her scant time off to dye her Perimeter Squad trousers in the laundry. She ate less at meals and smuggled food that would keep—fresh fruits, hard biscuits, and raw vegetables. From the kitchen, she requested and was given a stone water bottle, telling them she was going on a long hike. It wasn't entirely untrue, so she didn't feel guilty for lying. Only with Porridge could she feel any animation. She kept reassuring the emcrit that she would take it with her, but it still kept forming the sick dog, or the wet cat.

The day of Summer Festival was bright and sunny. A breeze kept the temperature comfortable. Sammna spent several hours with Porridge, trying to calm her own emotions so that it could revert to its true form, but it kept morphing into a shivering rat, cowering under her stroking hand. By the evening, as the full moon rose signaling the start of the festivities, and when everyone around her was excited and chattering, Sammna felt sick with anxiety. Finally, as her roommates began to get dressed in their best, she began to act out her stomach ache. Ellianne was disappointed but offered to stay with her.

"No. No. You go, Ellianne. I know how much you've been looking forward to the Fair. You go with Janess. Have fun. I'll be fine after I've had an early night and a good sleep."

Eventually—and with many protestations—her two best friends left. A surge of relief went through Sammna, but was quickly followed by regret and shame for deceiving and abandoning her sisters. Their loss would leave an enormous hole in her life. But she couldn't stop now. Her future as a boy seemed almost tangible. She bound her breasts flat, dressed in her adapted boy's tunic, and rolled up the dyed trousers and stuffed them into her backpack with a woolly cap, on top of the food. She enticed Porridge to get into the pack, and tried to impress upon it the necessity of staying quiet and hidden.

"I am a tiny, hidden bird. I am a tiny, hidden bird." She formed a mental image of a very small, black speckled ground bird, so camouflaged it could not be seen. She was relieved to see Porridge morph into an identical avian, huddled down under her trousers. She tied the top of the sack loosely. With a long look around the room she had shared with Ellianne and Janess for the last three years, she put her boots on, and slipped her long First Acolyte's robe over the boy's tunic.

Trying to look as nonchalant as possible, she strolled out of the Acolytes Hall and headed for the Fair. She mooched around the produce sale and the brew stalls. She watched with heightened awareness as men and women mingled. As the evening grew darker, she slipped behind one of the booths. Checking that no one was looking, she whipped off her female robe and stuffed it under the edge of the canvas. She pulled out the trousers, hastily settling Porridge further down in the pack, and silently commanding it to stay, to be still and small. She pulled the pants on and retied the sash around her hips. She spat into the palm of her hand and mixed a pinch of brown dirt to make a muddy mix. As delicately as she could, she darkened her eyebrows, lengthened her sideburns, and ruffled her hair, tying it back roughly. She shoved on the knitted cap.

"This is it, Porridge. Now I look like the boy I am," Sammna whispered. Taking a deep breath, he shook himself to loosen up, and stepped out from behind the stall with a longer stride, his backpack slung over his shoulder.

Sammna froze. Ellianne and Janess were right in front of him. Panicking, he swung around, looking for an escape. He swiped a tankard from the stall beside him and buried his face in it. So far, so good. They hadn't noticed. Taking a deep breath, he inhaled the froth and coughed wildly.

"Some boys should learn to slow down with the brew!" he heard Janess sniff. He kept his face down, and after a long breathless pause, risked a glance from under his eyebrows. Sammna sagged with relief as he saw his sisters move away. Then he stiffened as he felt a writhing movement from the backpack. Porridge was morphing into something bigger and more excitable than the little bird.

I am a hidden bird. A hidden bird, he mentally chanted. The sense of exposure made him put his head down and shrink in upon himself. He slipped through the crowd, trying to be inconspicuous but feeling that everyone was looking. He lurked around the crowd of boys standing on one side of the furthest dance floor. The wooden deck was lit by a group of wavering flame torches at each corner. The boys were vying for attention from a group of girls and didn't seem to notice an extra lad on the edge of their group. Sammna hung back, hoping to be unnoticeable in the shadows cast by the torches and the full moon.

He jumped as an elbow jogged him. "Go on, young fella. Ask one of those girls to dance. You won't get another chance for a whole year." He flicked his eyes up to a large man standing beside him. "I know how scary it can feel. But you gotta have a go. Here, gimme your backpack, I'll look after for it for you." A large hairy hand reached out toward him.

"No!" he squeaked, jumping backwards. "Ah," he coughed, remembering to deepen his voice, "thanks, but I don't want to dance.

I'm happy just to watch for now." As soon as he could, he started to fade backwards into the gloom.

Sammna had a terrible couple of hours, waiting for the boys to start moving towards the Gate for the return to the Male Enclave. He dodged away from anyone who came too close. Finally the group hanging around the dancefloor began to move. He pulled his cap down low and tagged along. He eavesdropped on everything they said, mentally composing a fiction of his evening, in case anyone asked. Several mentioned how much their fathers were keen to hear about their night's adventures. A father. He would have to invent a father, in case he needed one for his disguise. He kept his head down, and his eyes on the track.

"You look glum. Didn't you get a kiss tonight?" A gruff voice sounded right by his ear. He jerked in surprise and looked up. A large Protector, robed in black, was standing right in front of him, blocking the way. He could feel Porridge beginning to stir in the backpack, so he slung it off his shoulder and squashed it across his chest. A hidden bird, he thought urgently. The wriggling subsided.

"Well?" the Protector seemed as solid as a rock wall across the path. Prickling with apprehension, Sammna slumped in apparent dejection.

"Nah," he growled. "Got a dance, but no kiss. Tried, but she wouldn't." He tried to sound like the boys he had overheard a few minutes ago.

"Ah well, better luck next year." The Protector thumped a large hand on his shoulder. He squared up, trying not to buckle under the buffet. He nodded, and stepped forward. The Protector moved to walk alongside.

"What's your name?" The Protector seemed casual, but Sammna felt terrified by his continued attention. He'd never considered what he might call himself as a boy. It just hadn't crossed his mind that a new life as a male would also need a new name. Oh Goddess, what kind of names did boys have? The Gate didn't seem to be getting any closer, no matter how many steps he took.

"Me? Oh, I'm…" He covered his hesitation with a long cough. "My name's … Sammn…" He cringed inside, waiting for the Protector to grab him and raise an outcry. Instead, the Protector's hand reached out again and squeezed his shoulder. He clutched the backpack tighter, willing him to lose interest and go away.

"Salmon? Well, little fish, why don't you and I get together sometime soon? I don't have a partner, and you seem like a nice lad." His voice was softer, more persuasive.

Sam swallowed hard. He knew mono-sexual relationships were the norm in the Male Enclave, too. Hetero-sex only occurred at Summer Festival. But relationships and sex of any kind was not what he wanted, and certainly not now, not while trying to escape. I have to think like I'm a boy! He clutched the pack desperately against his chest.

"Ah, no thanks," Sam said, his voice cracking with the strain. "My father, err…" Sam couldn't think of anything further, his mind blank with fear.

"A bit strict, is he?" The big Protector moved even closer, his arm rubbing along Sam's. Terrified, Sam pulled away, squeezing the backpack for security. He felt scared to death that the Protector would touch him again.

"Err, yes! He is. We live…" A phrase from the conversation overheard last year between Gaia and the boy floated into his mind. "We live a long way out. He's a grazier. We don't come to town much." Go away, he urged silently. He could feel his heart thumping so strongly he thought the Protector must be able to sense it.

The Gate was looming over them. Sam took a deep breath and tightened his arms again. "Well, got to catch up with the others." He pushed forward, lengthening his stride. He sighed a huge gust of relief as the Protector turned aside, resuming his post by the portal.

With a sense of destiny unfolding, Sam stepped through the massive gateway. I'm through! I'm out! Wild swings of exhilaration, jubilation, and fear washed through him. Willing himself not to run, Sam hastened down the road. He put the backpack under one arm and hurried, so tense he could feel himself sweating. A few minutes later, by the light of the moon, he saw a track leading away on the left through the low scrub. The Expelled was that way, he knew from his map. He glanced back. There was no one behind him. Shaking, he leapt down the path. Now he began to run, crouching low, the stone water bottle in the backpack jouncing under his arm.

It felt like hours, or perhaps only minutes—no, definitely hours—before Sam reached a copse of trees standing shadowy in the silver light of the moon. Panting with effort, he pushed into the dark under their thick leaves. He stumbled through the undergrowth, feeling blind after the brightness of the moonlight. When he couldn't see out in any direction, he picked a large tree and sat down under it. He put his head down on the backpack, his breath heaving with mingled stress and relief. After a few minutes, he leaned back. The enormity of what he had done, of having escaped, of not having been caught by the big Protector, left him trembling and feeling sick. He breathed slowly, trying to calm down. The discipline of stilling his emotions made him remember Porridge.

With shaking hands, Sam undid the backpack. "Porridge?" he whispered. "Come on, Porridge." Momentarily, he wondered what form the emcrit would have taken with the enormous range of feelings he had experienced. Porridge was probably too terrified to morph at all. In the dark, he reached into the pack, feeling until his fingers contacted the softness of Porridge's fur. He held his breath, the better to focus on the sensation of the body in his hand. It wasn't moving. "Porridge?"

Frantic, Sam pulled the limp emcrit from his bag and began to massage it. He squeezed its chest, and stretched the front limbs, in and out, in and out. He felt the ribs expand as Porridge took one long deep breath. Sobbing with relief, he cradled the emcrit. But something was wrong. Porridge didn't feel right. It was thin, and its usually muscular body was limp and cool. And worse, he couldn't connect with Porridge's mind. He had felt that connection from the moment they had impressed. And now it felt ... as though it was blocked.

"Porridge, are you alright?" The emcrit didn't respond, but curled into its sleeping position, with its front paws over its eyes. Sammna continued stroking.

"Come on, little one. Cheer up. We've made it out. I'm a boy and we can go wherever we want."

He tried to inject some enthusiasm into his trembling voice, but Porridge didn't react. There was none of Porridge's usual representation of his mood, no sign of the huge range of emotions he was feeling—fear, elation, exhaustion, vulnerability.

"Can't you make yourself into a little chicken, Porridge? That's what I feel like right now. A baby chicken who has run away from the nest." He tried to grin, stroking the emcrit's back, but he felt close to tears again. "What will you make then?"

He felt a cold lump of dread fill his stomach. Porridge was not reacting to his feelings. Its form did not change.

"Maybe a rat? I feel like I've been a rat to Ellianne and Janess. What about that?"

Porridge did not morph, and continued to ignore him.

"Let's just sleep here in the dark tonight, and tomorrow you'll feel better. You must be exhausted. I know I am." His voice was shaking.

Sam prattled on, reliving the exhilaration and tension of the night as he recounted the events to Porridge. He shared out the food in the backpack, but Porridge didn't eat anything. Eventually, with the little creature curled in his lap, he drowsed into sleep.

In the morning, Sam set Porridge down on the ground as he tidied away any sign of their presence. He hoisted the backpack and discovered Porridge had squeezed in and curled up. "No, out you get, Porridge. You need the exercise after being stuffed in this bag all last evening."

He lifted Porridge out of the sack, and placed it on its feet. Porridge curled up, its head tucked down between its forepaws. Sam took a few steps, encouraging Porridge to follow. The emcrit did not move.

"Come on, Porridge. What's the matter?"

Porridge remained rolled in a ball. Sighing, Sam picked the emcrit up again, and cradled it against his chest.

"I'm feeling good today, Porridge. Can you tell? We're going to get to the Expelled, and live the life we've planned. I'm excited. Aren't you?"

Slowly, Porridge uncurled and looked at him solemnly.

"Porridge?" Sam felt a shiver of fear. "Are you able to change?"

Porridge leaned forward and licked him gently on the ear.

"You can't feel me anymore, can you Porridge?"

Porridge just looked at him.

Sam sat down, cuddling Porridge. He had a terrible knot in his stomach as he thought about effects of his choice.

"Oh Porridge, I never realized that becoming a boy would do anything to you! I thought it would only affect me." He stared off into the bush. He realized he hadn't really thought about anyone else. He swallowed painfully, as he realized the loss he had inflicted on Ellianne and Janess as well.

"What cost my identity, hey Porridge?" he mumbled. "I'm free, but I'm all alone. I'm scared. You seem to have lost the ability to morph, and I can't tell anymore how that makes you feel. I've made my sisters grieve, and all my friends. And I reckon there's no one else in the entire world who's changed like this. Nobody will ever know what it feels like."

Porridge turned around in his arms, and settled down.

"Not even you can feel what this is like. Oh, Porridge, I'm so sorry!"

Tears flooded down his face. He stared ahead, his gut clamping with guilt. He got up and began to trudge down the road, misery twisting his mouth, and Porridge in his arms.

Later, he felt Porridge wriggle. He put the emcrit down and waited while it relieved itself under a bush.

"What's going to happen to us, Porridge? Now you can't reflect my emotions, do we even have a bond anymore?"

He knew Porridge didn't really understand complex language; he was just voicing his thoughts out loud. So he was very surprised when Porridge looked over its shoulder at him, its expression somewhat startled. It waddled over to him, tapped him on the leg with one paw, and begged to be picked up. He felt a weak smile break the clamped tension of his face as Porridge cuddled in under his chin. Perhaps Porridge still loved him.

He helped Porridge into the backpack and started walking.

"How did this happen?" he wondered out loud. "I don't feel like a different person, I feel more like my real self. So how come you don't change anymore, Porridge? Which bit of me were you bonded with?"

He stopped as Porridge poked its head out of the backpack and put its front paws on his shoulder. It nibbled his ear, and looked back over his shoulder. It gave a shudder, then leaned forward and stared intently down the path.

"You're right. We can't stay here, and we can't go back."

He stepped forward again. Their future lay together somewhere out of the trees.

Penny Westhorp lives in Adelaide, Australia with her husband and two dogs. She left the professional article and journal editing business to launch her career into fiction. One piece of flash fiction was published in the January issue of In the Ranges. Currently, she is writing a dystopian trilogy and participates in a writing group. Her story, "Sammna & Porridge," won first place in Metamorphose's Kick-Off Contest in the Short Fantasy category.

Dangerous Dreams

Cecil Amore

FIRE WAS ALL I SAW around me. Along with the screams of children. I ran toward the screams, but then the sound changed and I altered my course. Time slowed and shadows danced around me until they solidified. Soon, two children were standing in front of me in the middle of the fire, unharmed. The flames licked their bodies. They giggled, looking at each other, and ran up the stairs. I chased them to a room that was familiar to me. By the time they stopped, sweat was dripping down my brow and I was panting due to the lack of oxygen in the air. The little girl walked over to me and placed her hand on my cheek.

She looked me in the eyes and said, "Why did you let us die, Fain?"

Before I could answer, the fire swallowed them and I fell through the floor into a different scene. I was looking at the house from the outside as it burned to the ground. As it burned, a hand touched my shoulder. I turned...

... And woke with a start. The tingling sensation that meant pain to me in this world covered my body, and the branch that is my makeshift bed because of the dangers that lurk below at night.

Getting off the ground with some difficulty, I began to rub my eyes and brush off the dirt and leaves off. Once I was sure nothing was broken and I was clean, I went back to the tree I fell out of and gathered up my bow and quiver, along with my sack. This dream made me wonder about my life before.

I didn't remember much of my life before I woke up on the forest floor. When I first arrived, I had no idea where I was or how I got there. I had wandered the forest for some time trying to remember something of my past. Soon, I noticed an emptiness that engulfed my sleep. No matter how hard tried I saw no dreams, but I felt like I was floating in an abyss. This abyss contained a darkness that froze you while you were there. Sometime later, I began to see a woman dressed in modern sophisticated attire. She always appeared calm, poise. Every time she visited, I would ask her name. She never answered.

She did show me about the place I was in—a place she called Legacy. She told me that everything around me was a dream that I created. Sometimes she would refer to me as an Architect from whom amazing things could spring. This stumped me. Until the day I confronted her about it.

"FAIN, ARE YOU AWAKE?" the woman's voice caressed me into consciousness.

"Yes. Yes I am," I replied.

"No you're not, silly," she replied with her girlish laugh. "Come on. Get up. It's time for your lesson."

Opening my eyes and sitting up, I notice that we were not in the darkness that I had come to know as the Boundary. We were in a meadow surround by various flowers. In the distance, a mountain range and a grandiose castle. I looked around for the mysterious woman but I could not find her.

"Fain, I used what little power I have to bring you to my realm." Her voice echoed from the mountains.

"Why did you do that, my lady," I asked, sucking in a breath as I took in the world around me. The beautiful fragrance of flowers mingled on the fresh air that surrounded me. Black and white roses encircled me in a meadow that sat between a large mountain range and a dense forest.

"It is because you have an important question for me," she said.

"How did you know that?" I projected my voice as she was doing.

"I know everything that happens in Legacy, Fain," she chuckled.

"Well then tell me, why do you call me an Architect?"

"At this moment I cannot tell you that secret but I do have a word of advice."

"And what is that?"

"When your Guide comes, do not reject its help. You are a strong boy who does not rely on others because of your past. Do not let that stop you from accepting help when you need it." There was a pause. All that passed through my mind was fear that she would fade before she could finish.

"My power dwindles fast, Fain. This is the last time we will speak for a long time; remember what I taught you and be patient."

As the Boundary began to take me back, I called to her, "Wait, do you know about my past?"

"Bye Fain," she whispered.

EVER SINCE THAT MOMENT, I made a world that allowed me to enjoy the simplicity of the world I left. I imagined the only thing that seemed to be inside my head: Sherwood Forest. The forest began to grow the more I thought of it until it expanded as far as my eye—which I enhanced—could see. Time went on and the world felt empty to me, so I added a small village near the majestic Major Oak of Fairwood. Along with these people, I thought of forest-dwelling animals and mythical creatures. I called the whole of my creation Fairwood.

Once the town was complete, the inhabitants branched out into different areas and a thriving world sprang from my thoughts and dreams. This thought overwhelmed me, yet gave me the idea to recreate myself. Rather than some lost boy who did not remember his past, I became the Fain, protector of the forest. The humans began to create folklore around me; stories about what I was and what I had done spread like wildfire between the villages. I was made into a demon.

Even with all the humans in my world, I still had no friends until a lone blacksmith moved deeper into the forest. Lexon was a brave man and became my best—and only—friend in Fairwood. He lost his wife and kids to bandits while he was out looking for firewood. He searched for these men, since the other villagers refused to reveal their identity. Many years had passed and he failed to find them, so he decided to settle down in solitary. That was, until he met me when I fell through his roof.

Once I was sure I had everything in my sack, I decided to head to Lexon's house. The path was simple for those who knew the forest. From the river where I slept, it took a fair amount of the day to reach his small cottage, with its quaint stone path leading up to the wooden door. An old friend gave this door to Lexon as a wedding present and engraved it with Lexon's family crest: an eagle clutching a heart in its talons. Lexon placed gold and silver within the engraving to make the door stand out.

He worked in the forge next to his cottage, where he made everything from weapons to nails for building. Something felt off about the place when I arrived at the front door. No candle was lit in the lantern that hung by the door. No smoke was coming out of the forge's chimney. These little things were odd because Lexon was a raging whirlwind of fury when it came to his forge and people not keeping it lit. The candle was for wayward travelers, such as myself, so they always had a place to go, unlike he did when he was a drifter. Seeing all of Lexon's quirks caused me to pause and wonder about my own, like packing my bag top-heavy. Before I could get lost in thought, I shook my head clear.

After a few knocks on the door, I decided to check the forge. Maybe he fell asleep with a bottle of whiskey in his lap. Opening the door was difficult since it was new and not weathered down yet, making me suspicious of what was going on since Lexon placed his doors out. I walked into the main room. Nothing appeared out of place. As I inspected the various assortments of tools, I notice the thin layer of dust that had collected. Running back to the house, I saw the scorched earth.

I pound so hard on the front door of the house that I thought it was going to come off the hinges. I waited a few seconds after knocking. Still no answer. I raced to the back of the cottage. The door lay on the ground as if it blew off its hinges. Slowly, I inched forward to the opening, readying my bow as I got closer. A crow suddenly flew out, scaring my soul from my body and making me shoot the notched arrow off into the distance. Readying another, I walked into the kitchen.

Inside was a mess. The kitchen table stood on its side, food scattered on the ground. Burn marks scarred the walls and floor in the kitchen. One mark trailed into the parlor. Cautiously, I followed. Something wet hit the back of my neck. Wiping it off with my hand, I looked up. Splattered above my head was a pool of crimson blood.

This sent me into a panic, coinciding with the creaking of floorboards and the scuffle of feet from the floorboards in the parlor room. The first thought in my head is that the murderer stayed behind. Maybe for the shelter. Maybe in the hopes of gaining some hidden item of value. Moving into the shadows of the dimly lit room, I began to skirt around the edge toward the front door. Just a few steps away from freedom, an icy cold blade touches my throat. The owner steps in closer, right up to my ear.

"You lost, Fain." The voice had the roughness of an older man.

"What are you talking about?" I tried not to move too much so that the knife did not cut me.

"The game. You lost the game and now your friend is dead." He chuckled in my ear.

"What did you do to Lexon?" I growled, now struggling against his grip.

"Ah-ah, you mustn't move too much or your throat might just open up."

"You would like that wouldn't you, you sadistic bastard."

"Why yes, yes I would. If you're offering I might just do it. But then again, where is the fun if I don't get to chase you first." He shoved me forward. "Run, little mouse, run."

Rather than running, I turned a fired the arrow that was still notched in my bow. It missed the man's head by a hair.

"Whoa, whoa, Fain calm down," he said attempting to dodge my arrows. "No need to kill me or destroy my house."

"This isn't your house. Now, tell me what happened to Lexon." I yelled, letting my anger come out like an icy dagger.

"I am Lexon, you blundering idiot." He threw open the door revealing, Lexon's face.

"Is that really you?" I said, mouth half agape.

"Yeah man, it is me so stop trying to kill me," he said, laughing as he walked over to me.

When he got within arms reach, I dropped my bow and punched him in the face so hard he fell to the ground.

"You fucker. What was the purpose of this," I yelled gesturing to the scene around us.

"You like it?" He smiled, looking at his workmanship with pride. "I thought I would have fun with you and try to scare you."

"Luckily, you didn't scare me." I crossed my hands over my chest and stuck out my chin.

"Oh is that right?" Lexon smirked. "And the fact that you nearly put an arrow through my head doesn't prove that you were scared?"

"I thought you were gonna murder me. What else did you expect me to do?" I said, defending myself.

"Touché," Lexon said with a smile on his face. "Well, you want to help clean this place up?"

"Fine, but only because you're my friend and I am sure you have something for me," I said with aloud groan of defeat.

Cleaning the mess in the parlor was relatively short, but once we got to the kitchen we knew we had our work cut out for us.

"Why did you make such a big mess," I complained, scrubbing the burn marks—which was just soot—off the walls.

"Would you have believed it if everything was still clean in here," he asked raising one eyebrow as he placed a bowl and the food back on the table.

"I guess you're right there." I picked up the over-turned chairs.

"You bet I'm right. Now help me clean off this blood on the ceiling."

Looking up at the crimson splatter on the ceiling, I remember the drop that fell onto the back of my neck. The thought sent a shiver down my spine.

"How did you get the blood up there and whose blood is it," I asked pulling a chair over to use as a ladder.

"Carefully." Lexon smiled. "The blood is a deer that I had for breakfast."

"Lexon," I said, looking at the man.

"Yeah, Fain," he said, looking up at me.

"You are one sick man," I growled, throwing some of the dried blood at him.

He laughed. "Well, when you live out here alone your mind gets a little twisted. Now hurry up and clean that. I have a job for you." He walked out to his forge, leaving me alone to work.

I began to chisel off the deer blood. It came off relatively easy, but not without some chunks of the ceiling falling out.

Shit, I thought when a large chunk fell out. Lexon was going to use me like a piece of metal in his forge. Where can I hide it? Oh man, oh man I'm gonna die when he gets back. I glanced at the open door, grabbed the largest chunks, and chucked them into the forest. Turning back to evaluate my work, my heart fell seeing all of the dust on the ground. Sighing I began to clean up the dust and burn marks.

By the time the sun reached the high point in the sky, I finished cleaning up Lexon's murder scene and washed up using water from a nearby well. After all the sweat, dust, and blood flakes came off, I made my way to the forge. There was a crash, and Lexon shouted curses.

"Lexon, you all right man," I said as I pushed the door open and entered.

"Yeah," He was leaning on his anvil, which was covered with a deer-skin tarp over it.

"What's under the tarp?" I asked, my curiosity getting the best of me, walking over to the anvil.

"Nothing," he replied, stepping between the anvil and me.

"What are you hiding under there?" I asked, trying to push past him.

"Nothing shrimp, now did you finish cleaning the house for me?" he asked trying to change the subject.

"Yeah," I said. "I cleaned up your mess and the rest of your kitchen."

"Wonderful," Lexon said distractedly. He walked over to his small desk in the back of the forge and grabbed a piece of paper. Returning back to his position in between me and the anvil he said, "Take this into town for me."

Taking it from him, I looked for an addressee but could not find one. "Ummm who is this going to," I asked.

"Take it to the gemstone merchant, and she will know what to do from there," Lexon said. "Now, you leave if you want to make it a good distance before the sun sets."

"Alright you ol' geezer I'll get out of your hair," I said walking back toward the door.

"Don't take too long. I need the item you are going for, so be back before the sun sets in two days," he said as I stepped into the noon sun.

IT DIDN'T TAKE LONG for the sun to slip under the horizon. Before it was completely gone, I climbed the tallest tree I could find and sat on a branch to watch it set. Every time I watched the sunset, it seemed like it was fighting against the will of nature to stay amongst the people and share its warmth and golden rays. As it loses the battle, the thought that haunts my mind is whether or not it will come back to my world and share all it has to share. What happened if it didn't come back? How would it affect my world? How would the whole of Legacy be affected? Where did the sun go to when it set in my world?

From there my thoughts turn to myself. I wonder who I am. What was my life before Legacy? Why have I begun to see fire in the Boundary? The lady never told me that dreams affected me in the Boundary. She never explained why I was here. Every day I am plagued by a life of no true meaning.

All of these thoughts plagued me as I watch the last sliver of light disappear into the Boundary.

ONCE AGAIN, I WAS INSIDE a house that was on fire. But this time I recognize everything from the carpet to the ceiling. I heard the screams of children coming from somewhere inside. I ran around, looking for the children. I checked every room downstairs. Nothing. Stopping to catch my breath, I heard the screams again. This time closer.

As the echoes of the screams faded, I walked toward the wooden flight of stairs and stopped. Looking up into the endless darkness that engulfed the stairs, I slowly put one foot onto the first step. Suddenly the fire was gone. I removed my foot and the fire returned, sucking all the coolness out of the air again. The screams reverberated throughout the house, then stopped suddenly. The fire disappeared and a shockwave sent me to the ground. I climbed to my knees and looked up into the brilliantly blue eyes of a young girl and the emerald green eyes of a young boy.

Both of the children were about six or seven and had similar facial features: pointed noses, endless freckles. The boy's hair was an unkempt curly brown, while the girl's was wavy and blonde. The sight of these two children sent a shiver down my spine and I wanted to vomit.

They shouldn't be alive!

I had no idea why this thought passed through my mind, but it frightened me nonetheless. Movement caught my eye and brought me back to attention. The young girl started to walk toward me.

She reached her hand out and said, "Why did you let us die, Fain?"

"I don't know," I said with tears pooling in my eyes.

Laughter soon filled the emptiness. It grew louder until I couldn't take it anymore. I curled up on the ground, covering my ears to protect them from their shrieking laughter.

"Why do you laugh at me?" I screamed.

" 'Cause you don't know what your future holds," the young boy said and with that both of them disappeared in a blistering inferno.

Floating in the Boundary's unending darkness, I pondered the answer. My future. What did that have to do with anything? I did not think there was a future to an existence in Legacy, unless you were one of the creations. The event that I first saw when I entered the Boundary this time also bothered me. The home reminded me of a distant memory.

A memory!

Is it possible that I could have a memory? The lady from my first days told me that I would lose all memories. I felt the Boundary begin grasping for my conscience. I fought with all my will to hold on to the memory, but it didn't take long for the Boundary to finally gain control over my thoughts and freeze my body.

Why I am not allowed to remember? I will never know.

The inside of my eyelids burned red and highlighted my veins as sunlight hit me. I stretched out, forgetting that I was on a branch, and nearly fell out of a tree again. Luckily, I caught myself and made my way down the tree. Then I started in the direction of the town of Lengale. It was the first city I created that thrived on its own.

It started as a couple of buildings with no inhabitants, because creating humans with personality was a difficult task. Every dream that was created in Legacy drained the energy of the person, so every time I tried to create a human I would be put into an extremely deep part of the Boundary. Eventually, I created a man and woman with personalities all their own. They were the founders of Lengale, but I soon had to add more humans. After adding a few more families, I left their world and lived in the forest.

That was where the legend of the forest dweller who robbed caravans began. I soon became a different thing to each town, once the people decided to spread out. Lengale soon became the capital of Fairwood and grew tremendously in a small amount of time. My original man and woman would become the first King and Queen.

Watching the town grow from a distance, I was able to influence the people through rumors and my powers as the creator. As time went on, I decided to fade out and let the world go on by itself. I ventured into the towns from time to time to catch up on the latest news.

To get into Lengale, most of the citizens went along Grimmwell Road, but I created many other paths to get in. The path from Lexon's cottage was the only one I did not make marks for. He preferred to be left alone and I didn't want bandits attempting to rob him. Finding the path was difficult since it was in the trees. Even the bandits were afraid to climb the trees because of the creatures—such as the Jabwroks, a lion beast with poisonous fangs and a deadly gaze—that lived in them.

Moving as swiftly as I could without falling out of the trees, I made it to the wall of Lengale sometime before the sun sat highest in the sky. I moved into the shadows to avoid being seen by the patrolling soldiers and stationed archers. Finding the entrance I created on my last run took some time from where I was hidden. The entrance was a warp in the wall that only I could see but would place any wanderer into the downtown part of Lengale. It was just behind one of the guards who was fixing some part of his armor.

Sliding farther back into the shadow, I tried to think of a way around the guard without being seen by the archers. That's when the idea of an invisibility ring hit me. Concentrating on that thought, I soon felt my energy drop, and the fabric of the world around me tightened and loosened. When I opened my eyes, a red ring lay on the ground. The ring was cold to the touch, yet looked like it was holding enough energy to start a forest fire. I placed it on my right ring finger and stepped out into the sunlight.

Hesitating a little, I continued walking until I reached the area of the wall behind the guard. Slowly stepping up to the entrance, I froze when the guard suddenly turned around. Holding my breath, I continued to step through the entrance until I was safely on the other side.

Releasing my breath, I turned away from the wall and began walking down the cobbled street to the gemstone merchant's shop. The street was empty except for a few early risers. I nodded to a jewel merchant. He walked past me without any acknowledgment.

"You could at least make some sign of acknowledgment, you fucker," I said turning around to face the man.

"Who said that?" the man said, looking around for the owner of the voice.

"Me. Are you really that blind that you can't see another person," I said walking up to the man.

"Where are you, you insolent brat?" the man said, his fear turning into anger.

"Right in forn—" I began to reply.

"Where are you?'

I decided to have some fun with the invisibility ring. While the man was standing there waiting for me to walk out of the shadows, I stepped behind him and pants him. Even us eighteen-year-olds enjoy juvenile tricks.

"Fuck," he blustered, his face blushing. "I'll get you for that, whoever you are."

He bent down to pull up his pants and I pulled his coat over his head and pushed him to the ground. When he got up, his face was redder than some of the roses I had seen in the forest.

"You'll regret this," he yelled, turning and stalking down the street. It was filling up with morning crowds.

I pulled off the ring and laughed at the man as he turned the corner, then made my way to the shop. It was harder to maneuver the street now that more people had begun their day. Every day before noon, the streets filled up with people looking to buy new items from the merchant stalls that lined the streets. Merchant voices yelled at every passerby trying to entice them to purchase their exotic items. It took some time but I finally reached the gemstone merchant's shop. The shop blended in with the buildings around it. The door was a simple wooden door and the shutters hung from their hinges in the front—probably from someone trying to break in. Upon entering the shop, my mouth fell open at the sight of all the precious gemstones.

It was a wonder the store wasn't robbed, with such a collection. I didn't see anyone at the counter in the back of the store, so I proceeded to look around. Most of the gems were in glass boxes and on ornate stands. The ones of immense value had special names and stood in thick glass containers.

One of the gems called out to me. It sat on the counter in a plain wooden stand. I walked over and read the nameplate: Mother's Eye. There was no price. I set the paper Lexon gave me down and examined the gem closer. It was a rather large gem—or at least from what I had seen—and it seemed to catch the light. The color was a rich golden honey.

The longer I stared at the gem the more I felt something pulling me toward it. I reached down to touch it.

"Don't," a woman said, a worried expression on her face when I looked up.

I screamed—I didn't realize someone was watching me—stumbling back and nearly knocking over multiple stands.

"You idiot, you're going to wreck my entire store," she said, running down the rest of the stairs.

"I'm sorry," I said hurrying to pick up what did fall.

"Leave that stuff alone, you will just break it," she said. She pushed me out of the way and picked the items up with a cloth. "You're lucky nothing broke or else you would be in some serious trouble."

"I'm sorry, ma'am."

"Name's Charlie, not ma'am." She stood and turned toward me. When I got a good look at her, I saw that she was no older than me. Her eyes shifted from brown to slightly green depending on the lighting, and her brown hair fell to her shoulders. She was lithe, which was surprising since city dwellers were usually bony unless they are upper class.

"Hey idiot, what are you gawking at?" Charlie said glaring at me.

"Nothing," I replied smoothing my hair down and leaning against the display rack portraying coolness.

"Right. You have a bit of drool on your chin," she said pointing to my chin.

I wiped it off as she asked, "So what can I do for you?"

"Umm... Oh hang on," I said, reaching into my pack for the note Lexon gave me. My eyes widened as I realized it was not there, but then I remembered that I placed it down earlier.

I walked over to the note and picked it up, waving it back at her saying, "Here it is."

She took the note from me and read it. Her face paled slightly as she finished. She turned and walked into the back room. When she returned, she had a box with her. The Mother's Eye was placed into the box.

"Here. Take it and leave now," Charlie said, staring at the store floor to avoid my confused gaze.

"Are you...."

"Just take it and go now," she yelled before I could finish.

I grab the box, place it into my pack, and left the store with only a glance back at Charlie. She was staring at me with tears welling up in her eyes.

THE SUNSHINE NEARLY blinded me as I stepped into the street. Oddly enough the streets were empty even though the sun had reached its noon point in the sky. I began to walk back to the warp I enter through until movement in the corner of my eye made me stop. I hear the shuffling of feet behind me so I pull my bow off my shoulder and notch an arrow as fast as I could. Spinning around I came face to face with the man from earlier.

"Remember me, you little bastard," he grinned. "I'm the one you decided to mess with. Well, I've got news for you that was a bad idea."

"What are you talking about," I said raising my bow as he moved forward slowly.

"Don't play dumb, you little shit," he spat. "I saw you just before I turned the corner. Thought that was a fancy little trick turning yourself invisible, huh? Well, it just got you into some deep shit."

He was now standing at the tip of my bow. He whistled and three other men joined him. I panicked and sought some escape. There was none.

Make one, a voice said in my head.

So I turned toward the smallest of the three and shot my arrow. It hit between his eyes with a thunk. Without thinking, I ran through the gap his fallen body left. I ran for my life.

"After him! Don't let him get away!" yelled the leader.

The other two lackeys caught up to me. One made a dive at my feet, knocking me to the ground. My head struck the cobblestones so hard I saw stars and nearly passed out. The taller of the two yanked me to my feet. Once I regained my footing and the world stopped spinning, I pulled out another arrow and shot. This shot went straight through the man's chest and struck the sign behind it. While regaining my senses and letting off another arrow, the rest of the group caught up to me.

Even as he fell, a searing pain shot up my left side. I turned, feet dragging on the stones, and faced the last man. He held a bloodied knife. This also gave the leader time to catch up to us. Knowing that I couldn't take the chance of shooting and missing now that there were two of them and one had a weapon, I ran toward the wall. Every step drained my energy. The man was nearly on top of me when I finally reached the wall and launched myself through it.

I land on the other side with a thud. I stood groaning but was knockback to the ground when the two men came bowling through the warp. The leader got up, followed by his lackey.

"You can't get away from me you bastard," the leader said into my ear.

"Hey, you there! Where did you come from?" A guard yelled.

I used the distraction, elbowed the leader in the face. It crunched under my elbow. I rolled to my feet and began to make a beeline straight for the forest. Stumbling across the open ground, I heard more shouts. Several arrows landed around me. Just before I entered the forest, a sharp pain rose from my thigh up through my spine. Looking down, I saw the shaft of an arrow protruding out of my right thigh. The adrenaline in my body allowed me to continue running from the men who begun their chase again.

It was a good thing that I knew the forest so well or else I would have been in even more trouble, but with all the blood loss I was starting to get dizzy. Hearing the men close behind, I climbed the tree as fast as I could. In minutes, one of the men was right under the branch I climb onto. He searched the area around the tree but stopped when he saw the blood at the base under my branch. He slowly raised his head until our eyes met. By this point, I already had an arrow notched and ready to fire, the moment he moved forward I fired. The arrow landed with a sinking squelch into his abdomen. It didn't faze him, so I shot another. It took five arrows to take him down.

As he died, I watch as the life drain out of his eyes before I fell out of the tree onto the ground. Looking up into the azure sky, I noticed that there weren't any clouds.

Only one thought crossed my mind before I passed out: Lexon what did you want with a magical stone?

Cecil Amore has been writing stories for ten years, but only in the past four years has the passion taken control. He started writing fantasy because it allows people to dream about things that you normally don't dream of as a kid. His runner-up story, "Dangerous Dreams," was inspired by his love of dreams.

A Walk in the Mist

Shelby Londyn-Heath

THE PATH WAS MUDDY and wet. Sam walked uphill, tugging his coffee bucket in the rain. The wild ginger plants exuded a fragrant tropical essence. The mist coming down the volcano was warm and moist, fingering its way through Sam's farming clothes. As the path wound upwards, Sam grunted with exertion. His sticky sweat mixed with the volcanic moisture, soaking his hair and face.

When Sam rounded the bend, he stopped. In front of him stood a pale figure, unmoving, a sculpted garden statue. She was naked with long blonde hair down to her waist. When she saw Sam, she moved closer to him. Wet curls framed her face and her large, swollen, blue eyes peered out at him. She walked toward him in silence, her bare feet oozing blood from the harsh lava rocks on the path, and her glistening skin goose bumps in the mist.

Sam stood still, clutching his bucket tightly... She kept moving toward him. To Sam's surprise, she walked past him.

"Wait a minute," Sam cried out. "Are you lost?"

She turned. "I was lost before you found me," she replied softly.

"But you're on my land. This is my farm. What are you doing here?"

"I live here." She turned and walked toward Sam again.

"What do you mean you live here? This farm belongs to my family. We've owned this land for over a hundred years."

She walked up to Sam and kissed him.

Sam trembled. He felt the warmth and softness of her breasts against his wet skin.

"I am the woman in your dreams, the one you call for in the pit of the night, in the morning strident air. I am in you and around you. I am the Goddess of your land. I bless you as you pick your crops. I am the wind whispering in your ears, and I am the sun burning your longing lips."

Her words frightened Sam.

She turned and walked down the path. Sam stood inert, fighting the unfamiliar feelings moving through his body and the animal signals lighting his brain.

Sam watched her long legs tread along the volcanic path. She walked sure-footed, like a mountain goat, edging over the craggy rocks created from the fiery eruptions of the land he proudly stood on.

Sam ran. He slipped and dropped his bucket. He jumped up. He ran until he was close behind her. He saw the beads of mist on her long arched back, and her firmness compelled him to edge closer to her. Sam suddenly longed to hold her beauty, to make her womanhood his fantasy-come-true. He felt like he knew her, though she frightened him at the same time.

When she turned towards him, he saw the shadows crossing her face. Her eyes were tight and half shut.

"Wait, where are you going?" Sam asked.

"I am a woman. I feed the roots, I nurture the buds."

"But where are you going now?"

"I am the conception that feeds your land."

"But I thought..."

"Step back. You can never find me."

"Why not?"

"Because to find me is to surrender to me. To surrender to me is to give yourself to my blood-roots."

Sam put his arms out to her. "Kiss me again," he cried out.

Her soft, long arms reached up towards the trees. "I am the light force that shields your rage. I am the mystery you fear at the edge of your dreams."

"Stop talking like that. I can be what you want me to be. Try me. Please kiss me again."

Her eyes opened wide as she moved towards him. "You cannot love me. You do not understand my blood coursing through the life of your land and the life of your soul. You cannot own my womanhood like you own your land."

Her face and body began to bleed. She stood motionless, a temple of blood turning her soft, white, skin into a fountain of rich, fertile life-force. Her eyes and hair flamed with the scarlet of unmet passion moving through her as the blood pooled at her feet. Sam watched in horror at the sight of large blood clots and coffee tree seedlings oozing out of her eyes.

He turned and ran. He could hear her laughter echoing behind him. "Why don't you surrender to me?" she called out as the leaves of the trees rustled in reply.

Sam ran down the twisted paths and old jeep roads leading to his house. He stopped running. He listened. Her laughter was gone.

A frightening silence moved in the wind. Sam felt an overpowering force pushing through him, and he sat down and sobbed with longing and emptiness.

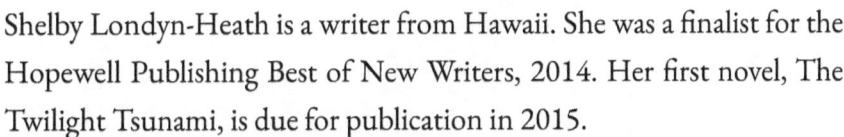

Shelby Londyn-Heath is a writer from Hawaii. She was a finalist for the Hopewell Publishing Best of New Writers, 2014. Her first novel, The Twilight Tsunami, is due for publication in 2015.

Life as a Goddess

R. H. Roberts

KATANA STRIPPED OFF HER torn black tights, tossing them in the trash with the ruined worlds before them. New worlds beckoned from her desk drawer. She stored scores of them there, waiting to be opened, brought to life and destroyed.

Nothing mattered more than those tights. The next pair didn't match her short dress, but she tugged the tan fishnets on anyway, knowing full well the dreams she'd have that night—sleepy villages full of fisherfolk, women weaving nets, children gathering shells and whittling bones.

She felt them crawl across her skin, their awareness expanding as she strode down the hall to her dinner meeting. Sure, it was a distraction, but she'd promised. And a Goddess doesn't break her word.

James stared as she settled into her chair at the round mahogany table. Her boss dressed beyond the height of fashion, wearing a silk hat and coat, even indoors. He trapped a moth flitting through an open window and lit its wings with a candle. It fluttered over the tables, dripping live embers until it crumbled to ash.

Early in her Goddessing, Katana had witnessed the horrors of living with cruelty. Her bitterness demolished world after world before the inhabitants ever gained sentience.

Never again.

"Some wine or a smoke, Katana?" James crossed the room, elegant in his understated way.

She refused. The alternative would be catastrophic—an intoxicated earth, a smog-ridden sky. Unthinkable. "Why keep asking me?"

He raised a brow and flicked charred moth parts from his impeccable suit.

Her left leg tickled, making her thigh twitch. She wouldn't scratch it, no matter how miserable she became. Tremors wreaked havoc on the villages in the fabric of her tights, but a scraping hand could wipe out civilizations. The exhilarating smell of brine filled her nose.

No one knew what worlds she wore, what lives she carried on her body. The shredded black hose from yesterday held a harsh empire—painful to wear, but still priceless. Some few souls had risen before that world fell apart. Another time, she tended hardscrabble natives. They toiled among stark gray ridges zigzagging down her legs.

James eased into the seat beside her, puffing his cigar while her co-workers gave reports. He reached beneath the table for her knee. Unfortunate, in this world, that even Goddesses were weaker than craven men. She smacked his fingers and he grabbed her hand.

At least he wasn't squeezing her leg. The fisherfolk were safe.

The meeting ended. The others left.

"Let me go."

He grinned, his dark eyes friendly. "Why do you resist me?" Before she could fight him off, he secured her hands in his fist then traced the netting up her thigh.

The scent of the sea intensified. Tears sprang to her eyes. Not from pain, but fear, springing from a world collapsing under the pressure of James' grasp.

He released her.

She fled to her room to assess the damage, inspecting the netting for frays or weavings unraveled. This fisher world called to her. She savored its sandy shores, the moonlight on the water, the taste of storms in the air. Generations had already lived and died on her slender legs, some shattered by untimely quakes, others simply grown old and weary.

A knock at the door.

James poked his head in while she smoothed down her dress. "I'm sorry, Katana," he said, although his glance flicked to her legs the way some men's eyes do. He sat across from her, not touching the netting that clung to her skin. "Who are you?"

"I am a Goddess. My choices matter."

He cocked his head, his mouth curved into a half-grin. "They warned me of girls like you." He stroked his silk hat and stood to leave. "I have worlds of my own."

As the door swung shut behind him, Katana's fishnets disintegrated and fell from her body. Sometimes even the best worlds died young. Glimmers rose from the dust. A woman, golden and strong. A man, warm and brown as the desert. They kept coming.

She'd mentored Gods and Goddesses before, but never so many. Not from one frail world, torn by the tempests of its own seas, the torments of the Goddess who carried it. They stretched and sighed, flesh and bone, risen from death.

Katana handed out leggings, cloaks, sweaters.

Her apprentices departed.

She opened her drawer and pulled on a new pair of tights, wondering about a world full of silk hats, belching factories, and burning moths.

R. H. Roberts lives with her husband and six children. In her spare time, she volunteers in schools and at church. Her speaking career includes creative writing seminars and presentations on Our Amazing Ocean. She loves anything with adventure, which heavily influences her writing. She returned to writing when pregnant with her fifth child, realizing she needed a creative outlet to keep her sanity. Her first novel is currently with agents. Her story, "Life as a Goddess," won Metamorphose's Kick-Off Contest in the Flash Fantasy category.

More from Metamorphose

Did you enjoy these authors? Get more volumes of Metamorphose.

Volume 1

Volume 2

Volume 3

Volume 4

Read full novels from Pangea Books.

www.ingramcontent.com/pod-product-compliance
Lightning Source LLC
Chambersburg PA
CBHW021033130626
46552CB00005B/1829